Becoming Tender in a Tough World

BECOMING
T·E·N·D·E·R
IN A
TOUGH WORLD

DENISE GEORGE

BROADMAN PRESS
NASHVILLE, TENNESSEE

ISBN: 0-8054-5079-3
Dewey Decimal Classification: 248.4
Subject Heading: CHRISTIAN LIFE
Library of Congress Catalog Card Number: 89-29553
Printed in the United States of America

The Scripture quotations in this publication are from the *Revised Standard Version of the Bible* copyright 1946,1952, © 1971, 1973 by the National Council of the Churches in the U.S.A., and used by permission.

Library of Congress Cataloging-in-Publication Data
George, Denise.
    Becoming Tender in a tough world / Denise George.
    ISBN 0-8054-5079-3
    1. Caring—Religious aspects—Christianity. 2. Sympathy—
Religious aspects—Christianity. I. Title.
BV4647.S9G46 1990
248.4—dc20
                                                    89-29553
                                                    CIP

For Peg and Ted
(The Reverend and Mrs. Edward Milley)
Two dear friends
who so beautifully embody
the tenderness of Christ.

Preface

I figure there are four basic ways we can approach life in a tough world.

We can fight it. We can try to become just as tough as the world is, being defensive and offensive and critical in our relationships, hiding behind a mask made of solid steel, and trying to be always in perfect step with society. This is the way of the world, the "Pull Yourself Up by Your Own Bootstraps," the "Become Number One," and the "Step on Anyone Who Gets In Your Way" style. There's lots of room for "me" in this life-style, but no room for God or anyone else.

We can become indifferent to it. Unable to be as tough as the world is, we can allow the world to make us unfeeling and uncaring. We develop into programmed robots. Life becomes one dull, dreary routine, holding few, if any, deeply satisfying relationships and no delightful surprises. In our indifference, we are like lukewarm water. We are neither hot nor cold. We just don't care. We approach God, others, and ourselves in the same manner: indifferently.

We can run away from it. In order to cope with the hurt and pain of a world tougher than we are, we can emotionally escape it. We can incarcerate ourselves in self-made jails, imprisoning our emotions and feelings and not allowing anyone, even God, to enter in. Or we can numb ourselves with drugs or alcohol so that we no longer live and feel, but simply exist in a sheltered and protected fantasy world of our own making.

These are sad and lonely ways to approach life. Within them, we never learn how really good life can be. And we never realize our God-planted potential. We never become the person God has created us to become.

But fortunately, there's another way to live in a tough world. *We can become tender to it.* It's the most meaningful way to live because it leads to the most rewarding aspect of life: genuine relationship. Becoming tender affects our relationship with God, with others, and with oneself. It is the way shown to us by Jesus Christ Himself, and it is by far the hardest way.

To be sensitive and caring and loving and vulnerable to a world that regards such character as weak and powerless and even foolish involves great risk. Nevertheless, I have come to believe that, even with the threat of being hurt and rejected and laughed at, becoming tender *in all ways* is the only way to live. And I am finding in my own life that it's well worth the risk.

☆   ☆   ☆   ☆

A book such as this involves the contribution of many. To my husband, Timothy; to my children, Christian and Alyce; to my parents, Bob and Willene Wyse; to my pastor, Charles Carter; to the Beeson Divinity School of Samford University and the Shades Mountain Baptist Church; to my family and friends and teachers, both living and dead, my deepest thanks and appreciation for your love, support, encouragement, inspiration, and expectation.

Denise George
Birmingham, Alabama

Contents

Whoever goes into public life has got to have a hide like a rhinoceros.

—Eleanor Roosevelt

1
Becoming Tough
in a Tough World

When I was a kid, I stepped off my school bus every day smack dab in the front yard of the neighborhood bully. Even though my house was just across the street from his, Tommy Turner wouldn't let me cross.

I still shiver when I think of this huge ten-year-old boy looming over me, his eyes red with anger, his nostrils flared and snorting. And I can still hear the devilish laughter that came from his throat after he had brought me to tears.

He was some tough kid, eighty-five pounds and built like a bull. I looked up at him the way a kitten looks at a German shepherd. Day after day, I endured Tommy's "torture," and when he finally let me cross the street, I ran home crying to my mother.

One day I decided that if Tommy Turner could be tough, so could I. I devised a scheme to outwit Tommy Turner and teach him a lesson he'd never forget.

It so happened that the previous Christmas Daddy had entered my name in a contest, and I had won a miniature, motorized Model T Ford. To a seven-year-old, it was some mean machine. It would soar at five miles an hour, had strong fiberglass fenders, and featured a gleaming front grille made of solid steel.

The next afternoon, after Tommy had teased me and sent me home in tears, I set my scheme in motion. I climbed into my car, hid in the garage with my little motor running, and waited until Tommy took his afternoon bike ride.

I saw the neighborhood's kids quickly scatter when Tough Tommy came out. I watched him perform his usual daring displays of bicycle toughness, riding in circles, leaping over manholes, and riding without hands. I timed it just right, and I caught poor Tommy on his fourth demonstration, riding with his feet high up on the handlebars.

Scared, yet chuckling inside at my ingenuity, I geared my Model T to fast-forward, gunned the engine to a full five miles an hour, and aimed the steel grille dead center into Tommy and his bike.

The hit was quick. The force knocked him to the street and scraped his elbows and knees. The steel grille bent the front wheel of his bike.

I can still remember the look of utter astonishment on Tommy's face. He disintegrated into tears and promptly pushed his crippled bike home.

For the first three days after "the hit," being tough felt pretty good. Tommy didn't harass me anymore at the bus stop. Good for me, I patted myself on the shoulder. I had showed Tommy I could be just as tough as he was. I wouldn't have any more trouble out of him, I thought.

On the fourth afternoon, however, Tommy's scapes had quit smarting, and he met me at the bus stop. Back to his own old self, he badgered me even longer before he let me cross the street.

Well, to make a short story shorter, Tommy became tougher and more unscrupulous, and I spent most of my evenings scheming up tougher and more unscrupulous ways to torment the tormentor. We both kept each other's eyes and shins black-and-blue. After a few years, my dad transferred with his job, and I said good-bye to Tommy Turner forever. It was not a tearful, "I'll-miss-you," auf Wiedersehen. In fact, I can distinctly remember sticking my tongue out at his front porch as we drove away.

Better Tough Than Sorry

I've always heard that if an elephant and a chicken get into a fight, the chicken had better be agile. Well, I was agile. Tommy was one tough animal. I, on the other hand, weighed forty-five pounds and was built like a pigtailed toothpick. I was so scrawny that the kids at school kidded me, "If it weren't for your Adam's apple and kneecaps, Denise, you'd have no shape at all!" It's hard for me to believe now that I could whip up even a tiny fear in Tommy. At any rate, every time I came charging unanticipated out of my garage in my mean machine, he bolted toward home.

When we moved into a new neighborhood, I couldn't wait to try out my newfound toughness on my next-door neighbor, a girl twice my size. Her name was Connie, and she had fingernails like Count Dracula. She used to file them into long sharp points, the better to sink them into my wrists. I believed she kept them painted bright red to match my blood.

The battle of the toughest began soon after we moved

in. We spent our long summer days catching grasshoppers in a nearby field and watching bullfrogs jump around in the rock-walled frog pond. I thought Connie was a pretty nice girl until I decided to take her prized grasshopper as my own. She turned on me, showed her fangs, and then punctured my two-inch wrist with her built-in arsenal.

That afternoon, as I licked my wounds, I set up surveillance from my kitchen window. I watched and waited until she squatted comfortably down by the side of the broken-glassbottomed frog pond to watch for bullfrogs. Then, unbeknownst to her, I crept outside, tiptoed to her backside, and with one hard shove launched her headfirst into the frog pond. I still remember the slime-covered sight of her as she emerged from the pond, eyeballed me, and then pointed all ten weapons at my throat. That was the shot heard 'round the neighborhood. The war had begun.

The Six Truths of Toughness

From those earliest memories, I learned several hard truths that I've sustained throughout my life.

One: When you fight, you get hurt.

Two: There's always somebody bigger than you.

Three: There's always somebody who has longer, sharper fingernails than you.

Four: Fighting is a no-win situation. Both lose.

Five: You can't have a satisfying relationship when you're at war with each other.

Six: When you go through life fighting, you must go through life fighting.

The Other Option

These six truths sank into me about the same time as Connie's fingernails. Pain, the teacher, and I decided once and for all it was time to stop pushing "friends" into frog ponds. There was another way to be tough. I didn't have to fight physically anymore. I could fight emotionally. Anyway, why meet the world every day in a lion-eating arena when you can just emotionally withdraw from the world? Seemed to make good sense. No more cuts and bruises. No one could see my battle scars now, because I would keep them on my soul instead of on my shins.

So I built a tough wall around myself. I made sure the rocks were thick and the cement holding them together was impenetrable. I barricaded myself in my self-made prison. Only a few times in those long years did I venture outside my cell to reach out to another person. This seemed the safer way. If I couldn't become tough and fight, I'd become tough and withdraw. Anyway, since I was basically a shy person, this way seemed easier.

Six More Truths

I learned some hard truths about living a life in prison, however.

One: Solitary confinement is safe, but it's lonely.

Two: It's dark in there. Prison dungeons shut out the loving sunshine of friends and family. Often the great Illuminator, God Himself, is not even invited into the cell.

Three: It's scary. In the brig, fears the size of baby mice become monstrous, human-eating rats handled alone.

Four: Unforgiven guilt and unrelieved stress become constant cell mates.

Five: Upon entering the bastille, prisoners lose their identity and become numbers. A number with no name can't love himself very much. Soon, self-esteem begins to drag the floor like a bothersome ball and chain.

Six: Prison bars block the freedom to become the creative potential person God plans for each of us to become. A sense of purposelessness encompasses you as you become accustomed to and comfortable with prison life. And purposelessness almost always produces hopelessness.

But the Greatest Lost Gift . . .

Tough and incarcerated, I gave up the greatest gift a human being can possess—a gift that becomes more meaningful to me with each day that passes. The gift is relationship. Genuine relationship. I'm talking about the deep, loving mutual relationship that begins with God, and spills over into family, friends, and oneself. A prisoner behind bars, even a self-imposed prisoner, cannot reach out to others in genuine relationship. Likewise, with the exception of a visitor or two who must stand behind a glassed, microphoned, and policed wall, others cannot reach in to the prisoner.

I would be almost thirty-five years old before I would fully understand that being tough, whether physically or emotionally, wasn't the answer to living in a tough world.

My Turning Point

Although I wasn't knocked down and blinded by a blazing light from heaven, like Paul on the Damascus Road, the "eye-opening" outcome was somewhat the same. My turning point away from sequestered toughness and into the *only* option for genuine relationship—triumphant tenderness—was a moment so intense and dramatically moving that it inspired my new journey, and, thus, this book.

My turning point into tenderness came late one afternoon as I came face to face with the toughest, meanest, wildest animal I believe God ever created. No, I'm not referring to my seven-year-old opinion of Tommy Turner, but to a sad and lonely rhinoceros imprisoned in the Zurich Zoo.

An Invitation to You

I'm glad you're reading this book. I pray that through these pages we can become friends. I invite you now to join me in my latest journey, a journey into the secret of genuine relationship, a journey into tenderness.

Forgive me when I grope for the right, but as yet undiscovered, feelings or words. I am embarking on a new journey here. I come to you not as one who has all the answers tucked neatly under her belt, but rather as a fellow searcher who daily struggles with serious issues concerning faith and relationship. Within the next chapters, you will probably learn more about me than is comfortable to me. Yet I come to you in vulnerability for the sake of communicating with you. Before you turn the page, please allow me to offer you an image to keep in mind as you read this book. Envision the image of a cross.

The cross is made up of a vertical line and a horizontal line. I see the vertical line as God reaching down to us and inviting us to reach back to Him. The horizontal line represents our reaching out to others and allowing others to reach back to us. At the point where the two lines meet, the very heart of the cross, stands One who brings it all together, the very center of all genuine relationships, whether with God, with others, or with ourselves. His name is Jesus Christ.

I look into the glazed eyes of the once happy, and now pitiful, creatures that exist behind man-made bars, and my heart hurts. I want to weep for those animals who once roamed so freely in their home-lands with animals of their own kind. They seem to have so little to live for now.

I know about cages, I think as I observe one lifeless animal after another. *I feel caged, too.*

2
The Tender Touch

The time was right for me to come face to face with an ugly, thick-skinned rhinoceros.

I had traveled through life a loner. By withdrawing from others to protect the tender inner me, I isolated myself from the love and enjoyment of people. Quietly I walked through life's rituals, those rites of passage such as school and graduation and dates and marriage and childbearing. But with each added year, the craving for genuine relationship grew keener.

By my mid-thirties, I was feeling lonely, isolated, and miserable as never before. The problem of my emotional withdrawal came to a head. I knew I couldn't go on like this, but I didn't yet know the secret of relating genuinely to others.

Little did I know that on one particularly depressing Monday afternoon the "secret" would hit me smack in the face like a Louisville Slugger. God had been waiting and the time was right, for He opened up a teachable moment for me that changed my life.

The Sabbatical

A few months before, we had rented out our house, our car, and our cat, and had stepped aboard a Boeing 747 to spend a full teaching sabbatical year in Switzerland, one of the most beautiful countries in the world. Not wanting to leave it behind, I transported my self-made prison along with me on that Boeing 747.

Upon arriving, the walls of my cell became even thicker when, in a matter of hours, I faced a culture I didn't understand and a language I didn't speak. Even the most simple everyday tasks proved impossible. I tried so hard to learn the Swiss-German language. But after ordering "chicken" and receiving green beans, and after calling a salesclerk a "pig" when trying to tell her my purchase was a "gift," I gave up. It was easier to keep my mouth shut. And much kinder to the salesclerk.

Being five thousand miles from home, having few English-speaking friends, and caring for two toddlers who had not yet been potty-trained left me feeling isolated from the entire human race. Timothy traveled most of the time in church history research. Day after day I stared unblinking at the dull gray walls of our tiny apartment.

Almost every day of those two-hundred-hour-long days reminded me of the day after Christmas. Depressing. The pain of isolation and loneliness, mixed with the stress of living in a foreign country and parenting almost single-handedly, seemed overwhelming.

During those long months, I withdrew into myself even more than before. I seemed to lose touch, to lose contact with God, other people, and myself. Never have I felt so empty inside. I felt as empty as a ballroom after the party is over.

Everyday life was painful. I hurt inside, and I felt depressed and distressed. I was surrounded on every side by breathtaking Swiss beauty, yet I closed my eyes and failed to see the exquisite rose gardens, aqua-blue lakes, and forests of snow-tipped pines. Often I didn't even bother to raise my eyes to behold the majestic Alps that towered high above me.

My energy level was also affected. It dropped to zero. I lost all ambition. I didn't want to get out of bed in the mornings.

I remember the morning when one of the children dropped a whole plate of scrambled eggs on the floor. Now I'm no "white glove tester," and I believe every home should have a few undisturbed spider webs in the corners. But whole breakfasts lying on the floor would ordinarily irk me. That morning, however, I didn't care. I sat on the sofa and stared at the crusty eggs most of the day, feeling no strength or desire to clean them up.

Feeling so sad and tired, I even found it hard to pray. I came to God at age nine, but never had God seemed so far away. I made no effort to reach out to God or to anybody else. I pulled myself snugly inside my private inner world and recemented the walls that enveloped me. My prison was becoming impenetrable. I craved affection and friendship, but, at the same time, I made myself believe I didn't need anyone. I just wanted to be left alone in my misery. And I just wanted to go home, back to the few familiar faces I loved.

Then Terrible Monday came, when I would learn a lesson that would change my life.

I invite you to relive this Monday with me. Truly, it was one of the worse days of my life and one of the happiest days of my life. Certainly it was one of my life's most significant turning points.

Monday, Monday . . .

The alarm clock goes off early this morning. I turn it off, and I wake from sleep with the thought, *Timothy leaves for Yugoslavia today.* I dread his going, for I will have no contact with him for weeks.

I fold the last undershirt and lay it in the suitcase. A quick kiss for each of us, and he leaves.

I feel unusually miserable. As I sit glassy-eyed on the sofa in our tiny apartment, I anticipate another day enclosed by the four drab walls. The apartment holds only life's bare necessities. The couch and chairs are wobbly and in shades of color weary to the eye. The walls are dingy and bare. The large windows in the front room open to an eternally busy highway, always noisy and heavily traveled by trucks.

I can stand the apartment no longer. I call two sleepy children and help them climb out of fuzzy "bunny suit" pajamas—pajamas so thick they can't feel the roughness of the woolen bed blankets. I slip them quickly into warm turtlenecks and padded snowsuits.

"Let's go to the zoo," I tell the children, who immediately jump up and down and squeal. I glance out the window and notice large, low clouds already spitting snow. We brave the cold Swiss wind and catch a trolley for downtown Zurich.

As I rock from side to side with the trolley, a toddler on

each knee, I repeat the safety rules for the fourth time. "Some of the animals are dangerous, so don't get too close and stay right with Mother."

I almost let myself feel excited about the zoo. I love animals, and I think the zoo will be fun for the children and will maybe even cheer me up. At least, it will be one more day to mark off the calendar—one more day closer to our return home.

As we walk the straw-strewn path and gaze at the rows and rows of locked cages, however, I wonder if coming here was the right thing to do after all.

I looked into the glazed eyes of the once happy, and now pitiful, creatures that exist behind man-made bars, and my heart hurts. I want to weep for these animals who once roamed free in their homelands with animals of their own kind. They seem to have so little to live for now.

"*I know about cages,*" I think as I observe one lifeless animal after another. "*I feel caged too.*"

The Rhinoceros

Within an hour of arriving, I am ready to leave. I take the children's hands and pull them in the direction we came. But, in a leap of mutual excitement, Christian and Alyce jerk away from me and run across the path to yet another confined animal.

I catch up to them, and I instinctively wince at the sight of the ungainly creature that stands separated from us by a five-foot-wide moat.

"Ugly animal," I whisper under my breath. "Ugly, ugly."

A rhinoceros, without a doubt God's most unusual and

hideous creation, stands gazing at us—probably thinking the same thoughts about us.

I edge Christian and Alyce away from the huge, repulsive animal who smells bad and who bears great horns in the most aesthetically unkind places.

But as I do, something happens that will stay with me perhaps as long as I live.

As if not wanting us to leave, the rhinoceros begins to stretch and lean forward. All the while he keeps his black beady eyes glued to mine. Then he stretches his neck and great head as far as he can past the moat with its double protective railings, and waits for my response. I motion for the children to stand back, for I do not know the rhino's intentions.

In an awkward and uncomfortable position, he continues to hold his head out to me. And for some unknown reason, I feel the urge to reach back to him. I stretch my arm as far as I can reach, and, with the tips of two fingers, I touch and softly pat the great horn on his nose.

Upon feeling my touch, the rhinoceros stands very still. Then he closes his eyes, and ever so gently sways his head from side to side as if reveling in the presence and attention of a caring other.

The Tender Touch

The touch. Human to rhino. Rhino to human. And I am touched, deeply touched by the action of this creature who makes both human and jungle animal run away at his very sight.

And my teachable moment comes. For at this touching moment, a thought strikes, a thought that etches itself forever on my mind. This wild beast, encased in a thick, protective hide, for the sake of relationship, has just shown me a tender heart. The rhinoceros so wants a loving touch, he literally sticks his neck out in vulnerability, exposes his true feelings, and, in doing so, risks humiliation and rejection.

The Paradox

How ironic the situation, I think as I stand at the moat and stare at him. *I, by nature, a tender human being, so afraid of being vulnerable and rejected, don a thick impenetrable mask and become tough. The rhino, by nature a tough animal, so wanting the loving touch of relationship, pushes aside his tough impenetrable mask and becomes tender.*

As far as any kind of relationship with a human being, this clumsy, repulsive animal has nothing going for him. Yet, in spite of the insurmountable odds, he takes a risk, becomes tender, and reaches out.

In his own way, this unconventional creature transcends toughness, and thus breaks the bonds of isolation and loneliness. He allows me to see the affection-starved personality that lives hidden beneath the layer upon layer of leathery prison.

Sticking One's Neck Out Is Worth the Risk

Over the last few years, I have come to realize more fully the lesson the Zurich Zoo rhinoceros taught me. Truly, it is a lesson I won't easily forget.

I am coming to understand that genuine relationship is built on tenderness, not toughness. It begins with removing the mask I wear, the tough impenetrable "hide" that I show to the world. For so often the mask conceals a tender heart that yearns for affection and knowing. I must also be vulnerable and take the risk of hurt and rejection. In essence, I, like the rhino, must "stick my neck out" in tenderness to another.

Rhinoceros tenderness. What a paradox! God used a rhinoceros to teach me about tenderness. What an unexpected and delightful sense of humor God has!

The Gift of Tenderness

The rhinoceros rendezvous happened almost three years ago. It came at precisely the right moment, a teachable moment, for its effect and impact on me proved astounding. My journey into tenderness began slowly thereafter and has led me down the path of some exciting discoveries.

For instance, I am discovering that in becoming tender to God, I am coming to know an amazingly close and fulfilling relationship with Him through Jesus Christ. In my becoming tender to family, friends, and others, my relationships have been transformed. I love people more, and, in return, I feel a deeper warmth of love from them reaching to me. In becoming tender to myself, I am becoming friends with a self I never really knew or understood or loved.

Needless to say, my journey into tenderness has been a revelation to me. No doubt, a lifetime of travel won't bring me to my final destination. But I am thoroughly engaged in and reveling in the journey.

Something Else Is Happening Too

As I move into genuine relationships, I am also discovering that the cement that holds my prison of isolation together is beginning to crack. I am seeing larger and larger shafts of light beaming into my cell. The lights are beginning to warm the soul inside the cell that for so many years has been hidden, cold, and lonely. Little by little I am spending more time outside my crumbling prison than inside. And life has taken on a whole new meaning.

I never went back to visit the rhinoceros. Freezing winter snows came, and after the spring "thaw," we left Switzerland and journeyed home. But in my dreams I imagine the rhinoceros still there, sticking his thick neck out past the moated railings, patiently waiting for the tender touch of a caring other.

Tough: Not Altogether Unwanted

Before we embark on our journey toward tenderness, please allow me to say a few kind words about toughness.

The word *tough* most often brings to mind undesirable ideals. In light of relationships, a tough person usually indicates a person who does not relate well, is strong-willed and difficult, rough, and even violent. We think of "tender" as being directly opposite of "tough."

Yet, in fairness to "tough," let me say that not all tough is undesirable. Depending on the context of its use, tough can also mean strong and durable, solid and sturdy, rigorous, secure, and substantial.

Partners in marriage, for instance, not only need a tender love but a tough, uncompromising love to keep the marriage together. Marriage cannot endure unless the love that holds it together is strong and durable, solid and sturdy.

I recall a mother of six whose husband drank a lifetime away. Somehow this woman had been given the gift of love so solid and sturdy that she endured a completely undependable, dependent husband. She had a tough love that enabled her to keep the marriage together, work full time for the sole income, and rear six children, all of whom have become healthy and nurturing adults. She did eventually help her husband overcome his problem, but only after many years of putting a tough love into constant practice.

Parenting also requires tender but tough love. It's no easy job (and that's the understatement of the century!) to rear a child from birth to adulthood. It takes a love that won't quit, a tough love, to stay with a "job" that requires twenty-four-hours-a-day, seven-days-a-week, fifty-two-weeks-a-year attention, guidance, and support; unbelievable financial investment; ultimate emotional commitment; maximum sacrifice of time and energy; and, for eighteen years or longer, offers no annual vacation!

I applaud and recommend this good use of tough. Indeed, in addition to marriage and parenthood, we also need toughness in other areas of our lives as well. One's faith in Jesus Christ must be tough, uncompromising, firm, and secure in order to live in Christ and also live in the world. To remain morally scrupulous, one must have tough and uncompromising values and beliefs. This is especially true today as we try to live a moral, upright life in a society that daily offers us a complete menu of tainted and selfish choices.

And, to remain physically safe in this world and to keep one's children safe, one must depend on a hearty dose of tough judgment and common sense.

It is the tough sound judgment that makes us bolt the doors of our homes at night, hold our young children's hands in public places, and refrain from picking up highway hitchhikers. Jesus warns us to be "wise as serpents" (Matt. 10:16).

I learned this lesson when Timothy and I were working in a church in Chelsea, Massachusetts, a rough and dangerous inner city on the outskirts of Boston. For some reason, I failed to use tough judgment, and, in doing so, I almost became the victim of rape.

At home alone late one afternoon, I unbolted and opened the front door without first knowing who knocked. A man, recently released from prison on rape charges, pushed his way into my home and threatened me. Scared to death, I somehow—and to this day I don't know how—talked him into leaving. I learned firsthand that as far as physical safety goes, tenderness should never be confused with naivete or foolishness or stupidity.

But, alas, we must save the "good tough" for another book, for in this book we will look at the other definition of *tough*, the tough that causes a person to fight or to become indifferent or to withdraw from the world. The tough that blocks genuine relationship and ultimately creates a sense of sadness, loneliness, lack of purpose, and lack of hope.

I know about this kind of incarcerated toughness. I lived there.

The Key to Becoming Tender

I have discovered that we can escape the prison of unwanted toughness. We can unlock the door that keeps us at arm's distance from genuine relationships. Each of us has access to the key. That key is tenderness. I believe Jesus Christ Himself, with an eternally outstretched hand, offers us the key to tenderness. It is the key that opens the cell door and allows us to walk in the sunshine of relationship with Him, with others, and with ourselves.

In its deepest sense, the love of God for man is that of a God who stoops down from heaven to enter into the world of men, with all its agony and pain, culminating in the grim cross of Calvary.[1]

—Alister E. McGrath

3
The Love Letter

I remember well the early August morning Timothy and I quietly slipped out of bed, packed everything we owned into our faded green Plymouth Satellite, and headed for Cambridge, Massachusetts.

We had spent the night with my parents; and, afraid good-byes would be tearful, we rolled down the driveway with our motor off at the agonizing hour of 4:30 a.m.

We soon discovered that Massachusetts is a long way from Chattanooga, Tennessee, our birth home. Neither of us had ever been so far from home before. And we didn't know what to expect up there.

Once we arrived, we quickly found out that Massachusetts is a long way from home in many ways, not just in miles. A strange land. We should have been suspicious at the very beginning of any place where 99.3 percent of its inhabitants had never heard of grits. (The first time we walked into a supermarket and asked for grits, the manager sent us to the foreign food section! And we found them there!)

It would be seven years before we packed up the same old Plymouth (by then a bona fide antique) and drove back to the South we loved.

The Letters

We stayed extremely busy during those long days. Timothy labored full time on two theological degrees, I pounded a typewriter day after day to pay for those two theological degrees, and we both worked hard in inner-city and downtown churches.

Those seven years were hard years, years when I felt lonely and homesick. We couldn't afford to go home for Christmas or Easter or for weddings or babies' births. At times, feeling so much inner pain, I didn't know if I could survive another day.

But we survived. Our deep faith in God sustained us. And Mama's love letters encouraged us.

My beloved grandmother, Alice Crane Williams, in spite of poor health and failing eyesight, painstakingly wrote one letter a week for the seven years we lived and worked in New England. They eventually totaled four hundred letters, each enveloped with a lot of love.

In her letters she shared the births of Emily, Tara, and Todd; described Alicia's and Ann's weddings; and filled in the details of each family reunion. But that wasn't the main reason she wrote. Above all, she wrote to communicate this message: "I love you. You are precious to me. You are an important part of the family. And even though I can't be with you in person right now, I am with you in spirit."

Mama's love letters came every Wednesday morning. Like a hearty bowl of hot vegetable soup on a cold and snowy day, they warmed my soul and gave me the encouragement I needed to make it through yet another hard week.

Seven years later, when we moved to Louisville, Kentucky, for Timothy to teach at The Southern Baptist Theological Seminary, the letters traveled with me. All of them. They were so precious to me, I held them on my lap for 1,200 miles, not risking them to the moving van.

As I held the yellowing letters on my lap, little could I imagine how they would reach out and continue to encourage me in the years that would follow.

God's Love Letter

Have you ever thought of Jesus Christ as God's love letter to us? Think of it. The human race was struggling for survival. The tough world had been alienated from God as a result of sin. Lost, afraid, and lonely, earth's entire populace groaned and wondered if it could survive yet another day.

In the fullness of time, when the time was just right, He came to us. The down-to-earth God. Why? He loved us. Perhaps He missed the evening walk in the garden. Perhaps He too yearned for a genuine relationship with His human creation.

So, He came. He strapped Himself with the burden of a human body, a body that got hungry, a heart that often broke with sadness, eyes that cried with the death of a friend, hands that held a hammer and became blistered from hard work. In becoming a human person, God learned firsthand our joys and our struggles.

He could have come to us a full-grown man steeped in wisdom and experience. Instead, He chose to come to us in extreme tenderness, a human baby, the most vulnerable of all living things. With the exception of two loving caretakers, a caravan of Wise Men, and a few humble shepherds, the world welcomed Jesus as a hungry lion would welcome a newborn lamb. He came a defenseless babe to a dark and dangerous world. God, Himself, became tender to us.

A Life of Tenderness

I feel so inadequate to reflect upon the God-man. I must agree with Saint Augustine: "I speak so as not to be silent." God, the Gracious Mystery. Words about Him seem so elementary. Yet so touched by God through Jesus Christ, we cannot keep silent, however clumsy our efforts to explain what happened on that starlit night in Bethlehem.

God came. And we learned two qualities about Him through Jesus, the One they called "Emmanuel" ("God with us," Matt. 1:20-23). We learned that God is for us, He loves us, and we are precious to Him. We also learned that God is present with us. He came so that we might enter into His family. And even though He is no longer with us physically, He is with us in Spirit.

Jesus came to a tough world to show us the way to God. It was with a human voice that He told us how to have a genuine restored relationship with the Father.

I once heard the beautiful story of a little boy who sat at his bedroom window one night during a terrible thunderstorm. He watched as the lightning streaked the dark night sky and the rain beat hard on the roof of the adjacent barn.

During the most frightening part of the storm a small lost sparrow flew against his bedroom window. Pelted by the fierce rain, the bird began to fly in confusing circles, crashing again and again into the window glass, searching in vain for a shelter from the storm.

Upset, the little boy ran out into the storm and tried to motion the bird into the safety of the warm protective barn. But the sparrow didn't understand. He only became more afraid and confused.

Finally, the boy grew exhausted. He had tried, but he couldn't help the bird find the way into the barn. And the small sparrow didn't survive the storm.

That night the little boy went to bed crying with a wish in his heart. *"If only, for just a little while, I could have become a sparrow myself, I could have shown the tiny bird how to fly into the barn."*

So God became a human being. For just a little while, He lived with us, and He showed us how to fly into the safety of the warm, protective barn. He came and He showed us how to find life itself.

But He Didn't Leave Us Here Alone

Jesus left us. And He no longer felt the beach's sand between His toes and tasted freshly fried fish with His closest friends. But He left us with the words instilled within our hearts: "I love you. You are precious to me. You are an important part of my family. And even though I can't be with you in person right now, I am with you in Spirit."

He sent His Spirit to encourage, to comfort, and to strengthen us in the many years that would follow. Reflecting on the everpresent Holy Spirit, the poet Tennyson would one day write: "Closer is He than breathing, and nearer than hands and feet."

We learned of God through Jesus Christ. And you and I learn of Jesus through the Holy Spirit.

In essence, God made Himself visible to us for the first time through Jesus Christ (John 1:18). Imagine. The blind man to whom He gave sight, the disciples, the rich young ruler, the woman at the well, the five thousand Jesus fed—all who looked into the eyes of Jesus looked into the eyes of God Himself.

For the sake of genuine relationship, the Creator tenderly gave Himself for His creation. "'Twas much, that man was made like God before, But that God should be made like man, much more," wrote John Donne.

Alister McGrath likens God's coming to two pieces of glass. The first glass is a window. Imagine being alone in a dark room when suddenly someone knocks a large hole in the wall. The sunshine streams in, and to your surprise you can see that a world exists outside, a world you had never seen before.

Jesus is the window into God. "He is the light of God who has come into the world to illuminate it, and who lets us see God. . . . God is made available for us in a new way."[2]

The second piece of glass, McGrath writes, is a mirror. Jesus is the mirror that reflects how life as a human being is meant to be lived. He showed us how to live tenderly in a tough world. The mirror also allows us to see ourselves as we will be one day, in perfect relationship with God.[3]

Why the Risk?

The Stepford Wives is a film I don't recommend. It's a story about some husbands who put their heads together and came up with an unusual idea. They would have their wives murdered and replace them with beautiful, flawless look-alike robots—robots who would love them, do what they told them to do, and wouldn't give them any lip!

This plan produces an obvious problem. What kind of marriage relationship can you have with a robot programmed to love you?

I have often wondered why God didn't make us robots, robots who would love Him, obey Him, and wouldn't give Him any lip. His creation could have been flawless.

Again, however, an annoying gnat appears in the middle of the lemon pie. Just what kind of relationship could God have with a world of programmed computers?

Love without the risk of being unloved is not really love at all. Relationship involves risk. For the sake of genuine relationship, our Creator took a risk.

God was serious about restoring relationship with His creation, a creation who defiantly disobeyed His rules. He loved us so much that He willingly died for us. Humanity nailed Him to a cross, and there Jesus died, suffering our punishment so we wouldn't have to. The great mystery of the cross. We cannot understand it with mere human minds. We can only believe it by faith.

Years ago, the message of the cross became very real to me in a profound yet childishly simple way.

I don't remember exactly what I did that day in the sixth grade to merit the punishment. I probably moved out of line, or talked in the rest room, or did something else against the school rules. At any rate, I was guilty of breaking the rules; and there I stood, a painfully shy, withdrawn youngster, facing a teacher who held a large wooden paddle in his right hand. A group of fellow students surrounded me to watch.

He held the paddle ready to spank me, a spanking I well deserved. I knew the rules, and I knew the punishment for breaking those rules. I was trying hard to keep the tears from spilling onto my cheeks.

Waiting for the paddle to come down on my writing hand, I heard a voice ring out beside me. "I want to take the spanking for her," offered a ninth grader I had never met before. He then stepped up beside me and took the paddling I deserved. As if yesterday, I can still see him willingly give his own writing hand to the teacher.

It's a crude analogy, but, in effect, Jesus did the same thing for us. We deserved the punishment for breaking God's rules. But Jesus stepped up beside us, willingly extended His own hand, and took our paddling for us.

The Invitation

The love letter God sent comes as an invitation to us. God humbled Himself to meet us where we are. He came to us in ultimate vulnerability. It only makes sense that He asks the same of us. In becoming tender to Him, we too must remove our acquired toughness and come to Him in vulnerability.

Relationship is a choice. It is shaped like a cross. God reaches down to us and allows us to reach back up to Him. Only then, I am learning, in genuine relationship with

God, can we reach out to others and invite them to reach back to us. God has knocked the hole in the wall and has given us a window into Him. And Jesus has personally handed us a mirror.

☆ ☆ ☆ ☆

On the day my beautiful Alice Crane Williams died, I couldn't go to her funeral many miles away. I was pregnant and ready to deliver my second child within days, a daughter who would be named after my beloved grandmother.

With my two-year-old son beside me, I sat in the yellow porch swing most of the day and cried. I missed Mama.

Then I remembered the letters. I climbed the attic stairs and found them—all four hundred letters tied with long blue ribbons that had held them bound for almost a decade.

I sat in the swing all weekend, and I reread the letters that had brought so much comfort and encouragement to me during the long hard years in New England.

And as I read them, I began to smell the deep, rich aroma of vegetable soup. The message of love poured forth from those letters and spilled into my life, once again giving me the needed encouragement to face the difficult days of surgery and recovery and new motherhood that lay ahead.

True, I would greatly miss Mama. But with her person and with her words, she had instilled within me the strength to face yet another day. And I knew that even though Mama could no longer be with me in person, like all the years before, she would always be right there with me in spirit.

Notes

1. Alister E. McGrath, *Understanding Jesus* (Grand Rapids: Zondervan Publishing House, 1987), 147.

2. Ibid., 110.

3. Ibid., 110-111.

He comes to us as one unknown, without a name, as of old, by the lakeside, he came to those who knew him not. He speaks to us the same word: "Follow me." And he sets us to the tasks which he has to fulfill for time. He commands. And if we obey him, whether we are wise or simple, he will reveal himself to us in the toils, the conflicts, the sufferings which we will pass through in his fellowship, and as an unutterable mystery, we shall learn in our own experience, who he is.

—Albert Schweitzer

4
Becoming Tender to Him

Not long ago, I read the touching story of four little South Korean sisters, aged six to thirteen, who decided to take rat poison so their parents would have enough money to educate their three-year-old brother.

Their family had little money. In fact, their father, Yang Taebun, supported the family on the equivalent of $362 a month.

The snapshot in the newspaper showed four knobby-kneed, dark-eyed, silken-haired youngsters standing side by side after a summer's day outing. They wore bleached white cotton dresses and smiled shyly to the camera. The smallest girl had a lovely round face framed by long black hair. She glanced up at the camera, but held on tightly to her mother's leg.

On the tragic Monday morning, they were found lying on the floor unconscious, the youngest girl already dead.

The event sent shock waves throughout South Korea. "The sad story touched the man in the street," reported the *Korea Times*. The love these girls showed, if even in a childishly mistaken way, led to an outpouring of love and sympathy from the country's first lady Kim Ok-sook and many others around the globe.

No Greater Love

How often love awakens love and tenderness awakens tenderness. A country was touched because four little girls loved their brother so much they were willing to give their lives for him.

"Greater love has no man than this," John 15:13 tells us, "that a man lay down his life for his friends." We hear about this rare kind of love so seldom that, even when it happens halfway around the world, it makes the Birmingham, Alabama, evening paper.

This is exactly the kind of love God demonstrated to you and me. He loved us so much that He gave Himself for us. God reached down to us in Jesus Christ and allows us to reach back to Him (Rom. 5:8). He sets the example. He shows us how to become tender to Him. We love Him because He first loved us (1 John 4:19). Charles Wesley penned it so beautifully in a hymn: "Amazing love! how can it be, That thou, my God, shouldst die for me?"

Knowing God

I believe the greatest gift God gives us is the gift of knowing Him. Not just knowing about Him, but personally, by His invitation, knowing Him. The apostle Paul wrote: "Indeed I count everything as loss because of the surpassing worth of *knowing* Christ Jesus my Lord. For his sake I have suffered the loss of all things, and count them as refuse, in order that I may gain Christ" (Phil. 3:8, italics mine).

It took me a long time to understand his words, but I would now agree.

How can we know God? We must come to Him as He

came to us, in great tenderness and vulnerability. We come to Him as trusting babes. We look to Him as our Father, a Father who greatly loves us.

I can remember the beauty and innocence in my children's faces when they were babies. When I nursed them, or bathed them, or rocked them, large blue trusting eyes would stay glued to mine. They would watch me with such peace and contentment, knowing I loved them, knowing that I kept them in mind and heart throughout the day. They seemed to know I would meet their needs, and they trusted my gentle and loving touch.

We can look to God, our Father, in the same way—with trusting eyes kept on Him, and with peace and contentment of soul, knowing He loves us, knowing He keeps us in mind and heart, knowing He has promised to meet our needs. We have simple childlike trust in a loving Father, a Father who has gone to great lengths to show us His unending love.

Jesus told two stories that have helped me to know God the loving Father better. They have also helped me to love Him more. I believe they speak to the person who is coming to God for the first time, as well as to the person, like myself, who has been far away from God and who has recently come back to Him.

The Loving Shepherd

Imagine this scene: A little lamb wanders off from the flock in the middle of the night. The other ninety-nine lambs are huddled together under the watchful eye of the kind, protecting shepherd. Every hour or so, the shepherd stands up. With his long staff he counts each lamb, touching each animal gently on the head. Each lamb awaits and anticipates his gentle, caring touch. Ninety-seven, ninety-eight, ninety-nine . . . the one hundredth lamb is missing.

The shepherd counts again, and still, lamb number One Hundred is nowhere to be found.

Lamb number Seventy-Three punches lamb number Twenty-Seven. "Ol' One Hundred's playing hide-and-seek again!"

Number Twenty-Seven, however, taking the situation far more seriously, speaks up: "But what if he's lost and can't find his way home? He might die out there all alone!"

The shepherd knows the dangers that await a small, innocent lamb. He knows it's a tough world out there, filled with wolves and other hungry creatures who would enjoy a midnight snack of fresh lamb chops.

Without hesitation, the shepherd sets off looking for the lost lamb. He searches and calls and checks under each brush. Finally, after an exhausting search, he finds the frightened lamb. And the good shepherd rejoices. Number Twenty-Seven was right. One Hundred was lost and he couldn't find his way back home. The shepherd gently hoists lamb One Hundred on top of his shoulders and takes him back to the safety of the flock (Luke 15:3-7).

What is the story's take away for the reader and hearer? God is the Good Shepherd in this story. He is the One who goes out for you and me, the ones who have wandered away from His flock and into the grips of a wolf-infested world. Just as every lamb is important to the shepherd, every person alive is important to God. Knowing that I am important to God changes the way I feel about myself.

For if the Creator of the universe thinks I am important, then that gives me infinite worth.

The Loving Father

Jesus gives us another image of God as the loving Father.

Allow me to dress up the story, a story that, no doubt, you've heard and read a hundred times.

A brooding teenager says to his semiretired father: "Pop, give me what's mine and let me have the keys to the family car. I want to go to New York where the action is and whoop it up awhile!"

The kind father feels hurt, but he hands over his car keys and his American Express card.

The kid does, indeed, whoop it up in the Big Apple. His credit card gets him into ritzy night clubs, five-star restaurants, and the best downtown escort services. "This is the life!" he shouts from the window of the Waldorf Astoria.

But, at the end of the month, his credit card bill comes due. He can't pay it off, and he can't get any more credit. The bouncers at the hottest night clubs bounce him out, the escort services no longer supply him with an evening's entertainment, and the elegant meals become fast-food hamburgers. He is kicked out of his hotel, and his gas gauge registers empty. To make a long story short, he's in a mess.

In the next scene, we see the teenager living over a hot air grate in Harlem. He's cold and hungry. His dad's car no longer has a battery, hubcaps, or stereo speakers. Late in the evenings, he scrounges through Central Park's trash cans looking for supper.

One night, as he pops into his mouth the remains of a thrown-away hamburger, something dramatic dawns on him. In other words, with the taste of spoiled lettuce-pickles-onions-cheese in his mouth, he experiences a rare but teachable moment.

"Hey man, this is not fun. I'm not having a good time anymore," he mutters to himself. He "gets his head on straight" and begins to feel genuinely sorry for the way he's treated his father. As he chews, he thinks about home, and he comes up with an idea. "Maybe Pop would let me come back home and work around the house. You know, I could carry out trash, clean out the garage, wash the supper dishes, that kind of work." He shivers at the thought of such work, but he has made up his mind.

With stale meat between his teeth and apprehension in his heart, he thumbs a ride home. During the long trip home, he rehearses his speech to his father. "I'm really sorry about all this, Dad. I'm sorry about the car, and I'm sorry about your Dun & Bradstreet credit rating. I don't expect you'll let me come back home, but if you will, I'll straighten up. I'll work hard and pay you back for all the damage I've done. I promise."

Once or twice he almost decides not to go back home, fearing his father won't take him back. And rightly so.

"Thanks a lot!" he calls to his ride and steps onto the edge of the driveway. He dreads facing his father, especially with a new foot of tangled hair and a three-month-old beard.

But, to his utter astonishment, there waiting in the yard to meet him is his father. In fact, he's been coming out to stand in the yard for months waiting for his son to come home.

When he sees his skinny, haggard, long-haired son, he doesn't walk to meet him. He runs to meet him. He wraps his arms around him, kisses him, and welcomes him back home.

"My boy's come home! My boy's come home!" he calls to the neighbors. The neighbors peer over the fence and whisper to each other: "I wonder when that rotten kid's going to wipe out his father again and hit the road?"

The boy's older brother doesn't like it a bit, but the father throws a backyard barbecue and gives the prodigal a new leather jacket and keys to his own turbo-engined Mustang (Luke 15:11-32).

Indeed, I've embellished the story more than a bit, but the message is still there. It's a message that, even the one hundredth and first time I hear it, makes goose bumps on my arms. God is not only the Shepherd who goes out into the far country to look for the lost lamb. He is also the Loving Father who stands in the yard and waits for His child to come back from the far country. God is the Loving Father who runs to meet His son or daughter when the prodigal gets tired of whooping it up and decides to come home.

We are dear to the Father, and He misses us when we are not with Him. He lights the lamp in the window; He sets our plate at the supper table. And even when we "leave" Him, or neglect Him, or fight Him, He stands in the yard and waits for us to come back home.

Not only does the loving Father wait for runaway prodigals to come back home. He also waits for drifters to come home too. Drifters aren't the rebellious ones who demand their inheritance and head for the far country. Drifters are those who forget who they are and whose they are. They allow the details of life to creep into their life of faith, and they just slowly drift away.

No Longer the Same

When the lamb and the teenager enter into the safety of home, they are somehow changed. The world outside no longer holds an attraction. They now prefer to stay close to the family hearth, a hearth that gives warmth and safety, tenderness and love. A hearth that becomes the center of their lives. A hearth they never want to move away from again.

When we come to God for the first time, and when we come back to God for the last time, we are no longer the same. We are changed. Jesus becomes the Lord of our lives, and all the promises and parties and bright lights of a tough, tempting world no longer mean much to us. We become like the cocooned moth who wakes up one sunny morning, and, looking at himself in the mirror, discovers for the first time he's changed. He has wings. Beautiful, brilliant wings that give him freedom to leave the cocoon and fly around in the fresh air and sunshine.

If you could put a minuscule microphone to the butterfly's mouth and ask him some deeply probing and investigative questions, he might exclaim: "What? Go back to that dark cocoon? Why would I ever want to go back to that prison when I'm free?" You might even hear him singing as he flutters away, "Free at last! Free at last! Thank God, I'm free at last!"

Becoming Tender to Him

You see, the butterfly has experienced a transformation. He has become what God created him to become. God didn't create him to be an ugly gray moth all his life. God always could see the butterfly in him.

In a sense, we too are butterflies. But only in Christ can we find our wings. Only in Christ can we experience transformation and become what God created us to become. We become new creatures in Christ when we decide to become tender to Him. "Therefore, if any one is in Christ, he is a new creation; the old has passed away, behold, the new has come" (2 Cor. 5:17). What exciting news for us! When we come to Christ, we are . . . and we are becoming.

Just how do we come to Christ? Simply. Like a child. In complete openness, vulnerability, and teachability.

We come to Christ in deep humbleness, truly seeking reconciliation for our broken relationship with Him, truly sorry for our wrong choices, and eager to respond to His words "Follow me."

The famous line, spoken some years ago by Ali McGraw to Ryan O'Neal in the film *Love Story*, comes to mind here. "Love means never having to say you're sorry."

I couldn't disagree more! Relationship involves saying we're sorry. Only then can forgiveness come. (When once asked how many times we must forgive our brother, Jesus replied, "Seventy times seven." Timothy forgave me that many times during our first week of marriage!) Truly, Ali and Ryan, love means having to say you're sorry.

Becoming tender to God involves our having to say we're sorry. He forgives us and then He makes us His new creatures. When we decide to follow Him, we turn away from our former moth life. And He begins the transformation, a change that will help us to become the butterflies He created us to become. True, He accepts us just as we are when we come to Him—moth wings and all—but He surely doesn't expect us to stay that way. He sees the butterfly in us while we are still moths.

Becoming Real

When we come to God in all tenderness, God makes us real.

"What is REAL?" Velveteen Rabbit asks his toybox friend, Skin Horse.

"It's a thing that happens to you," answers Skin Horse.

"Does it hurt?" asks Rabbit.

"Sometimes," answers Skin Horse.

"Does it happen all at once?" asks Rabbit.

"It doesn't happen all at once," says Skin Horse. "You become. It takes a long time. . . . [But] once you are Real you can't become unreal again. It lasts for always."

Velveteen Rabbit became "real" because Boy loved him, and in return, Rabbit loved him back.

Skin Horse was right. Becoming real doesn't happen overnight. "Generally," Skin Horse admits, "By the time you are Real, most of your hair has been loved off, and your eyes drop out and you get loose in the joints and very shabby."[1]

We become real because God loves us, and, through the price He paid, He offers us the opportunity to love Him back. Christ makes us real when we come to Him, yet becoming real is also a journey. A long journey. Paul saw it as a race, not looking back but always pressing forward toward the goal: Jesus Christ. "Not that I have already obtained this or am already perfect; but I press on to make it my own, because Christ Jesus has made me his own. Brethren, I do not consider that I have made it my own: but one thing I do, forgetting what lies behind and straining forward to what lies ahead, I press on toward the goal for the prize of the upward call of God in Christ Jesus" (Phil. 3:12-14).

Becoming tender to Him is a journey in which we are being changed into His likeness. We are becoming as He is (2 Cor. 3:18).

And once we become real, we can't become unreal again. It lasts for always. For once we've had a taste of God's forgiveness and have come into genuine relationship with our Creator, even if we decide to imitate the prodigal and step outside the family home, even if we start to slowly drift away, something in our soul will stir us back. For love has awakened love and tenderness has awakened tenderness, and we can never, never forget the warmth of the family hearth.

Note

1. Margery Williams, *The Velveteen Rabbit* (New York: Henry Holt and Company, nd), 4-5.

Trust in the Lord with all your heart
and do not rely on your own insight.
In all your ways acknowledge him,
and he will make straight your paths.

—Proverbs 3:5-6

5
Dragon Scales

Teach me to do thy will,
for thou art my God!
— Psalm 143:10

I am discovering that in order for me to *know* God and to live *in Christ*, I must come to terms and deal with a generously endowed portion of strong will.

No doubt, this mighty will developed within me as I was formed. I am told that the whole hospital hall outside the delivery room heard my birthday screeches immediately upon my arrival.

Those screeches, I might add, knew no cessation for the following thirty-five years! I had an inborn desire for power. I wanted to control everyone and everything, including myself and my circumstances.

Whether fighting as a youngster or withdrawing as an adolescent and adult, I've had a self-will that just wouldn't quit. It has always wanted complete control of my life. Its greatest desire is to become president of the world.

For three and a half decades, words like *surrender, obedience,* and *submission* were simply not in my vocabulary. I considered them good religious words, but to me they denoted weakness. I was tough, and my strong will belonged to me. For years it was the rudder that alone guided my ship.

I'll Do It My Way, Thank You

I was like the old strong-willed farmer who was determined to pull the loaded wagon to the top of the hill, even if the wagon had no wheels. He pulled and pulled, advancing only an inch at a time, all the while getting nowhere and making deep furrows in the ground. But the poor farmer never stopped and looked inside the wagon. For if he had, he would have discovered four good wheels that would have made the difference between uphill struggle and conquering strength.

The farmer's wheelless wagon reminds me of the clumsy double stroller Timothy and I rigged up and pushed all over Switzerland.

Afraid our two preschoolers would tire from walking, we tied two strollers together, put one child in each side, and, side by side, we pushed.

Needless to say, the long afternoon hauls would exhaust us. Two forty-pound robust children, forty disposable diapers, two tins of Tidy-Wipes, fifty-five graham crackers—you get the picture. The stroller was heavy! And I'm not talking about rolling along on level ground or pushing up molehills. I'm talking Alps!

"Push faster! Push faster!" Christian and Alyce would call. Poor huffing and puffing Timothy and I would push white-knuckled and straight up the mountains of Switzerland until we stood almost prone.

I look back on those afternoons and ask, "Why in the world didn't we make the children get out of the stroller and help push?" I mean, after all, since birth neither child had for one minute stopped trying out for the 1998 Olympics. For fourteen long, continuous hours each day, they hopped, jumped, skipped, and bounced through life. The energy in the tip of Christian's little preschooler finger would have quadrupled the accumulated and potential energy of both Timothy and me together.

So there, strapped in the strollers, were Christian and Alyce, fussing, wiggling, and wanting to be free, two energy balls that could have easily made the difference between up-Alp struggle and conquering strength.

A Lifetime of Uphill Struggle

Until recently, I spent a lifetime pushing up-Alp all by myself. Even though I lived emotionally withdrawn and wore a pretentious smile of peace and tranquility, I was dictated by a tough will that wanted to direct its own uphill paths. If only I had stopped and looked and listened, I would have seen the One who stood beside me, the Source of conquering strength Himself, patiently waiting for me to ask for His help.

Waiving the Will to God

Whenever I think of the strong-willed, self-guided Christian, I envision a person covered with tough green dragon scales. Dragon scales may represent anything that blocks, or at least hinders, genuine relationship with God. They are like thick prison walls that shut out the Light.

No matter how hard we pull, we ourselves cannot remove the scales with mere human strength. They have been attached too long. They are embedded too deeply. Human efforts are useless in pulling them off. Only God can remove them, one by one, until we are completely rid of them.

I believe a strong will is one of my many dragon scales. God has recently begun to pull those scales off, and only now am I beginning to allow Him to mold and shape my will to make it useful to Him.

Dragon Scales!

Dragon scales! How we Christians yearn to be rid of them all! C. S. Lewis's boy-turned-dragon, Eustace, from the *Chronicles of Narnia*, knew about dragon scales. Eustace tried three times to take the dragon skin off himself; but each time he thought he had pulled it off, he discovered he hadn't really. For more dragon scales lay beneath. Only the sharp claws of Aslan the lion (the story's Christ figure) could tear off the scales that had long imprisoned Eustace within its scaly skin.

Dragon-scale removal is a long process, a necessary process, and a process that usually hurts. It means a change of life, a change of thinking, and a dedication/rededication of oneself to Christ. A total change of life almost always proves painful.

"The very first tear [Aslan] made was so deep that I thought it had gone right into my heart," cried Eustace.

"And when he began pulling the skin off, it hurt worse than anything I've ever felt."[1]

Letting go of and giving up my dragon scale of a strong self-will has been one of my many recent turning points of faith, however. Truly, the Christian who yearns for genuine relationship with the Father must be "descaled" from many things, but first from his own strong self-will. Becoming tender to God means giving up the power-hungry will. It means waiving the control of others, the control of circumstances, and the control of oneself to God alone.

Letting Go and Letting God

"*Thy* will be done," Jesus taught us to pray to the Father. Perhaps that is the hardest part of the Lord's Prayer for us to pray and really mean.

This idea of letting go, the very substance of faith itself, took on a vivid picture one day as I sat at my kitchen window and looked out on the small wooded mountain in our backyard.

I noticed two trees side by side, one short, one tall. A squirrel climbed to the lowest branch of the tall tree and sat there perplexed. He wanted to move to the next tree, but the highest branch of this particular tree was several feet beneath the tall tree's lowest branch.

He had a problem. He sat at a standstill. Then he did something that surprised me. He simply let go of the branch he clung to, dropped several feet, and then grabbed for the small tree's highest branch. Needless to say, during the letting go I caught my breath and waited for the crash. But he made it. It didn't seem to surprise him that he made it. And he went on his merry nut-collecting way.

Since that episode, I've watched other squirrels take the same unusual action at Squirrel Drop. I can honestly report to you that not a single squirrel has yet fallen to the ground on his furry little tail.

It's an elementary example, but I believe faith is like that. We can hold onto our strong will and remain exactly where we are, not moving forward, not maturing spiritually. A standstill. Just hanging onto the same branch, out on a limb, for a lifetime. Or we can let go of the strong will we cling to, give it up to God, and trust Him that the next branch will be there to catch us before we hit the ground. By letting go of our will, by trusting God completely, we can move to the next level of spiritual maturity. But first, we must trust Him enough to simply let go.

Indeed, following Christ means a lifetime of letting go. How do we do that? It started this way for me.

The Transforming Prayer

"Lord, take my will and make it yours. No matter what it takes, shape it and mold it until my will becomes your will and I become the person you've created me to be. Let me trust you and acknowledge you in all my ways. Teach me to do what you want."

Not long ago, I prayed that simple prayer and I gave my strong will to God. Since then, when I've felt the forceful will creep back up onto my shoulders, I've prayed the prayer again. I have felt His strength working in me, making me more useful for the work He wants me to do. I've a long way to go, but I believe I'm in process.

A Horseshoe in the Making

I often feel like a shapeless piece of steel being pounded and hammered into a horseshoe. With each hit of the hammer upon the anvil, I slowly and painfully take on a little more shape.

In many ways it would have been easier not to offer my steel will to God. It would have been easier to remain shapeless. The anvil is cold and the hammer is hard.

But can the anvil be any more cold than the cross? Can the pounding hammer hurt any more than the penetrating nails?

Because He sought to be shaped by the Father, I do too.

Jesus said, "Follow me." If we truly love Him, we will seek to follow Him. If we seek to follow Him, we must give up anything that would hinder discipleship. The first step in discipleship is tenderly handing Him our will and allowing Him to be the sole rudder of our ship.

The Carpenter

When we let go of our will and give it to God, God starts to work on it. He is like the skilled carpenter who saws, shapes, polishes, and makes something useful of us.

Several years ago my dad semiretired from a business career and set up a woodworking shop in his backyard. I have since been amazed at the splendid pieces of furniture that have come from his shop. Spice cabinets, oak shelves, and a handsome desk—all products of his skilled hands—fill my home.

A few weeks ago I visited his shop. I watched him take some long strips of rough lumber and run them through a planer. He then sawed them into shapes, sanded and polished them, and nailed them together into a tall cabinet with large drawers.

I couldn't help but become somewhat theological while I watched him take useless rough wood with no shape or purpose and make it into something useful and beautiful.

Amidst the flying wood chips and sawdust, I mentally envisioned God as the Master Carpenter and myself as the
rough piece of lumber. With skilled hands, He was shap-
ing and sawing and sanding my will into something
(someone) who will one day be useful to Him. (How appro-
priate that God should have chosen carpentry as His
earthly occupation!)

Could it be that within each piece of rough wood lives
and breathes a polished work of art? Yes! But only a
skilled carpenter can bring it forth. It takes a Michelan-
gelo to release the exquisite statue of David from a hunk
of discarded and unsightly granite.

The Artist stands waiting with tools in hand ready to
release us, to mold us, and to make us into His exquisite
works of art. But . . .

"Follow Me"

To those He called by the seashore one day, Jesus spoke
two simple words: "Follow me."

Over the centuries, volumes have been written on the
meaning of those two words. To follow someone means to
come after him, to literally walk behind him in his steps.
It means modeling or patterning one's life after his life, to
emulate and imitate his every action. To follow someone
completely means to conform to his ways, and to respect,
listen to, and obey his words and example. In essence, to
follow demands 100 percent time, energy, and thought. In
this regard, we can't follow someone part time. This type
of discipleship requires a whole new way of thinking and
living and acting. We must give ourselves completely to
the one we follow and become his full-time student.

I believe God requires this kind of response of anyone who would follow Him. Does that sound like bad news, 100 percent devotion? You might be thinking right now: "That's impossible! How can I give God 100 percent of my time, energy, and thought when I have an income to earn, a family to feed, a house and yard to take care of, income tax to figure, church work to do? In this twentieth-century rat race, I barely have time now to brush my teeth!"

Good question. And one morning I was given some insight into a possible answer.

As is my usual practice, I woke up very early, made a cup of coffee, and sat in my "morning meditation chair." I had many things going through my mind, however: my son's soccer practice this afternoon, my daughter's Teddy Bear Parade this morning, the income tax to finish and mail, stacks of laundry to wash. Caught up in mentally scheduling my day, I forgot to pray—the main purpose of my early morning commitment.

I drank the last sip of coffee, rubbed my eyes, and looked at the clock. Time to get the kids up, dressed, and fed for school. But before I got out of the chair, I saw something in the room I had never seen before. I noticed that the morning sun streamed into the room through the windowpanes and cast the shadow of a cross on my wall. Of the four doors inside the room, the center of each bore the design of a cross. The glass in my cherry secretary had small panes of wood all shaped like crosses. I was surrounded by images of the cross!

All morning, as I dressed the children, cooked breakfast, washed clothes, and accomplished numerous household tasks, I noticed that in every room of my house, wherever I looked, I saw the shape of the cross. I have become so aware of it that I've begun to look for it, in the doors, in the windowpanes, in the furniture, in the sun-cast shadows.

Bringing the Cross into the Center of Our Lives

Later that day a thought struck me. Could it be that we can keep the cross of Christ always within sight as we go about our busy days? Could we, in the midst of earning an income and feeding children and figuring income tax, keep ourselves so aware of and surrounded by the cross that we can follow Christ in total devotion and obedience 100 percent of our day?

Many times I have heard and read the verse in Proverbs 3:5: "Trust in the Lord with all your heart. . . . In all your ways acknowledge him." But never have the words "in all your ways acknowledge him" held more meaning.

Insight visited me a second time and asked: If I could be constantly aware of the cross and bring Christ into my everyday life, would it change my everyday life? How would my every day be different if, before I said a word or took an action or made a decision, I asked myself these questions: What would Jesus have said; what would Jesus have done; what would Jesus have me decide?

That would be quite an experiment, wouldn't it, being always filled with the Spirit of God? For instance, would I figure my income tax differently if I brought Christ into it? Would I be a better parent to my children if I imitated Christ's response to the children He lifted on His lap? Would I regard housework in a better light if I followed Jesus' example of tenderly feeding a multitude or washing His disciples' dirty feet? Would I better choose my

words if I said only those words I believe Jesus would
have me say?

How would my life be suddenly transformed if I awoke
each morning looking for the cross, spent all day listening
for His voice, and went through my day waiting on tiptoe
to obey His words of instruction? How would my life be
suddenly transformed if I let the Father control my heart
and life, if I put my feet directly into each footprint of His
step and walked behind Him every moment of every day?

If that were possible, can you imagine how your life and
my life would be changed? Can you imagine the volumes
about Christ we, through our words and actions, would
speak for Christ to others?

Is it possible?

I don't believe it can happen overnight, for complete
submission and obedience to God must be learned and
practiced day by day. But, yes, I believe it can happen.
And the good news is this: "[God] *gives* us what He demands of us, [He] *provides* the obedience that He
requires."[2]

Discipleship requires two people: the leader and the follower. In this case, the Leader gives the one who follows
the strength and obedience needed to be a loyal follower.
We simply let go and give Him our will so that it might
become His will.

Jesus asks us to love God—"love the Lord your God
with all your heart, and with all your soul, and with all
your mind, and with all your strength" (Mark 12:30).

If we can do that, if we can totally surrender ourselves
to Him, if we can make Him Lord of our everyday lives,
then God will do the rest. He will make us one with Him,
and He will remove any dragon scale that gets in the way

of our oneness with Him. One day we will be able to say with Paul: "It is no longer I who live, but Christ who lives in me; and the life I now live in flesh I live by faith in the Son of God" (Gal. 2:20).

The Results of Everyday Faith

When we make Christ the Lord of our lives, we might find that several things will begin to happen.

First of all, we will look at life differently. We will see crosses all over our home and office and grocery store and beauty shop. Everywhere we go we will see the cross of Christ. We will develop a keen new awareness of the One who walks directly in front of us, the One into whose footprints we place our feet. That initial awareness of Him will make us want to discover a deeper awareness of Him. Studying the Scriptures, listening to good sermons, and asking faith questions of fellow Christians will fill us with rare new excitement. We will become enthusiastic about our newfound faith—so much so that we won't be able to keep it to ourselves. Our full cup will run over and spill onto all those around us. We will be forever hungry to learn about God through the One who came to introduce us to the Father, Jesus Christ.

Other changes will begin to take place too. We will begin to schedule our days differently. Spiritually meaningless jobs will capture our spiritual eye. We will look at them more critically, and we may even decide to change jobs that hold no purpose except for the earning of money. Or we may take on new part-time or volunteer jobs that spiritually enrich us and others.

Old ways of living will probably also go down the drain.

For instance, we may exchange an evening of a TV miniseries for a neighborhood Bible study. We may take a second look at our role as husband and father, wife and mother, church member, relative, and friend, and seek new ways to make those relationships more significant. We may begin to give up less meaningful activities and friendships to spend more meaningful time with those we love. We will begin to unselfishly put ourselves in third place next to our first-place God and second-place family and friends. Indeed, becoming tender to God in our everyday living will change the priorities of our everyday living!

For sure, we will no longer be so quick to laugh at the insensitive office joke. Nor will our ears be able to tolerate gossip and unkind remarks made about others. Witnessing another's little white lies (even unspoken), deliberate deceitful actions (no matter how trivial), and even a negative, downcast personality will cause us to inwardly revolt.

We may wonder what in the world is happening to us! What is, in fact, happening to us is a little word called *consecration*. It's a word full of power. It means that once we give our lives and hearts and whole beings to God, we are no longer the same. We will start and continue to separate ourselves from those things and those people that would block our new relationship with God.

Consecration is a new commitment, a devotion, a sacred vow, an act of the will. And it cannot begin until we hand our will to God and say, "Yes, Lord, I will follow you."

If You Love Me . . .

Jesus said: "If you love me, you will keep my commandments" (John 14:15).

Obedience means acceptance, allegiance, compliance, conformity, and submission. Obedience is having a spirit of teachability. We are open to Christ, we make ourselves teachable to Christ because we love Him. Obedience is doing right even in a world that doesn't value doing right.

I learned obedience and teachability in a new eye-opening way when we moved to Alabama.

I have loved everything about Alabama since we moved here. The state is beautiful, the people are unusually friendly, the climate is comfortable. But the Alabama-bred fire ants are a menace.

I had never met a fire ant face-to-face before moving to Alabama. They are amazing creatures, ranking right up there with the mosquito and wasp. They cover the ground with foot-high and foot-wide nests, and they just dare you to come within ten feet of them. While on a self-induced nature study, I poked around their nest one afternoon and unexpectedly discovered their distinctive bite. It stung for two weeks. (Someone named them appropriately.) I have learned since that if I want to avoid the inevitable bite of the fire ant, I must stay away from its nest. Simple lesson learned in one afternoon.

In considering our obedience to God, sin is the fire ant. God gives us our boundaries. They are written in plain view, in His Holy Word, the Bible. We have even been given the wisdom and clarity of the Holy Spirit to help us know right from wrong.

I have discovered that I can have wonderful freedom

within those boundaries. But I also have discovered that if I decide to deliberately step out of those boundaries, then I suffer the consequences. No, God doesn't zap me with a bolt of lightning; but sin does. When I exercise my free will in disobedient ways, I bring heaps of trouble onto myself. I believe God allows me to suffer the consequences of sin much as a good father would allow his child to learn lifelong valuable lessons in the same way.

I can remember when my children each hit eighteen months old. As if an alarm had gone off in their little biological clocks, they each immediately incorporated the word *no* loud and clear into their limited vocabulary.

Oh, how they would test their limits! (They came by it naturally.) I explained exactly what they could and could not do as each trying situation arose. Within their boundaries they could have a great time. But whenever they stepped over the invisible line I had drawn for them—a line they could see very well—they would end up falling off the chair they weren't supposed to climb or cutting themselves with the scissors they weren't supposed to use.

I also remember suffering the consequences of disobeying my dad when he distinctly warned me not to put my five-year-old hand on the bright red stove burner. Exerting my will, sirens inside me screamed: "I will! I will! You just watch how I will!"

Needless to say, I did. And the stove burner separated the top layer of my skin from the bottom layer of my hand. And I can tell you that, to this day, I wince at the very sight of an electric stove!

One More Word . . .

And that word is *sanctification.* Sanctification happens when we surrender our former tough world life for a new life, a life of tenderness toward the Father.

As we mature in our Christian faith, life becomes very different. We become set apart for a special calling, the vocation of serving God. And we begin the process of becoming sanctified.

Sanctification is the state of growing in divine grace as a result of Christian commitment.

We begin to strive toward what is good and holy; we begin to stay away from what is bad and evil. We walk the road to purity, purity of the whole self—body, soul, and spirit.

Paul encouraged the new Christians at Thessalonica: "May the God of peace himself *sanctify* you wholly; and may your spirit and soul and body be kept sound and blameless at the coming of our Lord Jesus Christ" (1 Thess. 5:23, italics my emphasis).

Sanctification means keeping our eyes always on God, being always aware of His presence. Sanctification "will cost an intense narrowing of all our interests on earth, and an immense broadening of all our interests in God," wrote Oswald Chambers.[3]

Sanctification causes us to concentrate intensely on God and strive to become one with Christ, no longer pushing our wheelbarrows uphill alone, but tapping into the conquering strength available to us all.

Notes

1. C. S. Lewis, *The Voyage of the Dawn Treader* (New York: Collier Books, 1952), 90.
2. D. M. Baillie, *God Was in Christ* (New York: Charles Scribner's Sons, 1948), 144.
3. Oswald Chambers, *My Utmost for His Highest* (New York: Dodd, Mead & Company, 1935), 39.

Pain is a great paradox. It is replete with anomalies and contradictions. It can be creative and destructive; it can ennoble and embitter; it can protect and destroy. . . . It is an effect of evil but can also be a means of good.[1]

—Norman Autton

6
The Rock

Let the words of my mouth and the meditation of my heart
be acceptable in thy sight,
O Lord, my rock and my redeemer.

—Psalm 19:14

When we decide to become tender to God, we must decide to become tender to Him in *all ways,* even in the
meanest of experiences, the experience hardest to com-
prehend: our pain.

Pain, the cruel yet effective teacher. Our faith can be
tested as never before by the fire of pain. Does God cause
our agony? No. God does not cause our pain. Yet, for some
reason we can never know, in some mystery we could never fathom, God allows us to experience pain.

And when I listen to the lessons of the hurt and pain of
life, when I become tender to them, accept them, and seek
to learn from them, when the hammer beats the hardest
on the anvil, the horseshoe of my soul begins to take
shape as never before.

Physical pain, mental anguish, emotional suffering—
they are all part of the human package. They have created upheaval within the human soul since the beginning

of time. No doubt, the experience of pain has brought many Christians to their knees in urgent contemplative prayer and yet has also produced more atheists than could be counted.

The Pain of Loss

In many ways and in many hours, pain has walked beside me as an unwanted companion. Not long ago I experienced an hour of great emotional suffering when at last I revisited the empty home of my deceased grandparents.

I'd like to share that experience with you now.

Going Home

The rain taps on the hood of my car as I pull through the opened gate. Already the sick feeling in the pit of my stomach begins. My children sit quietly in the backseat as I drive into the driveway and stop. I hesitate. Tears well in my eyes and start to spill onto my cheeks. I shake my head in disgust and promise myself I'll never come back here again.

Mama and Papa's farm. My birth home. The beloved white frame house with the tall, stately pointed eaves is falling apart. Neglect and decay have taken over. Last week's storm blew off the awnings of both back and side porches. They lay in the yard broken and twisted. Only a few of the large hickory trees are still standing.

"Let's get out of the car!" Christian and Alyce impatiently shout in unison.

I fumble with umbrellas and wonder why they are so eager to see such ruin.

Together the three of us walk around the large front yard and I notice how tall the grass has grown. Weeds have taken over the rose gardens that once so elegantly encircled the house. Cars have repeatedly hit the fence that encloses the yard and have knocked much of it down.

Inside the house is even more depressing. It seems so empty. Most of the furniture has been moved out and scattered. Some of the walls are cracked and leaning. The wallpaper is discolored and torn in places. I see the shadows where rows of family portraits once hung and the empty hook where Mama hung her housecoat. The house is little more than a hollow shell of a treasured remembrance.

The pain of death surrounds me. Death has squeezed the once vibrant life out of the house. The familiar voices I used to hear no longer speak here. No loving words, no kind wishes greet me at the back screen door. No children play games on the living room floor anymore. Friends no longer telephone to say hello. No light, no sound, no movement. I stand still, very still, enveloped by the pain of deathly silence. I leave the house unable to bear another moment of the torture.

We start to go. But before we step into the car, something happens. As if handed a living album of rich, warm, and almost-forgotten memories, I am instantly whisked back through the years. My mind, resisting the distressing present, voluntarily steps into the past. To my surprise, I am a little girl again.

For the next few minutes, as I stand in disbelief, I relive in extraordinary detail the delightful hot summer days of my childhood on Mama and Papa's farm.

No longer do I see the empty, dying farm suffering from three years of damaging rainstorms and indecision about its future. But I see life, an alive and pulsating farm years before death took Mama and Papa away from it. I again feel the love they had for this house and yard and thriving gardens. They opened its doors wide, and, with vitality and healthy pride, welcomed all who would enter in. Each time I walked through its gate, I felt as if I had stepped into paradise itself.

All of a sudden, a happy little girl bounces across my path and runs toward the bright red henhouse to collect freshly laid eggs for breakfast. I immediately recognize the girl with the long dark-brown hair and matching eyes, the girl the family so lovingly calls 'Nisey. For I am that little girl who stops and winks and smiles at me from my childhood of long ago.

But she doesn't stay long. She sees her grandmother walking through the rose gardens and darts to her side. She is an inquisitive child who must know the name of each rose and how it grows. She walks hand in hand with her grandmother, talking enthusiastically and deeply about life and death, family and God.

"Mama, where did God come from?" I hear her ask.

"Now, 'Nisey, we don't know the answers to questions like that," Mama whispers.

The next minute the youngster is standing beneath the hickory trees gathering nuts in the apron Mama has tied around her small waist.

A gentle, damp wind blows through my hair, and from across the yard I hear the clear, familiar voice of my grandfather.

"Come here, 'Nisey. I've got an ice-cold watermelon just waiting to be cut!" From out of nowhere run five more young grandchildren. We stand in line waiting for our slices. I breathe in the sweet fragrance of a newly cut melon and feel the cold juice running to my elbows.

The little army of grandkids follows Papa into his vegetable garden. Papa picks a large tomato from the strong vine. "Have you ever seen tomatoes grow that big?" he laughs.

I close my eyes and take a deep breath. It's no longer cold and raining. I am enjoying the hot summer day of so many years ago. All of a sudden, I catch a whiff of cornmeal-coated okra frying on the stove and fresh butter pound cake baking in the oven. I tiptoe to the kitchen door window and peek inside. There at the sink stands Mama in her flowered cotton housedress, peeling potatoes for vegetable soup.

Time picks up now, and the many hours I spent at my grandparents' farm race through my memory like a charging locomotive. In one second, I am surrounded by aunts and uncles and cousins opening Christmas presents in the living room and spooning turkey and dressing onto holly-trimmed plates. In another, I am searching out Easter eggs in the tall grass Papa has purposely let grow for the hunt. In another, I am sitting on a stool in Mama's kitchen reveling in her presence and buttering her homemade corn bread.

How good it feels to step into the past. Change seemed to come so slowly then. I perk up my ears, and once again I hear the gentle rain tap the aluminum porch awning. I hear the familiar strains of Papa's guitar as we gather around him and sing. I begin to hum one of the many songs he taught us: "The wise man built his house upon the Rock, the wise man built his house upon the Rock, and the rains came tumbling down. . . . "

I feel sad when the memories begin to fade. "A time to

weep, and a time to laugh" (Eccl. 3:4). I whisper the verse from Ecclesiastes as I sense the album of treasured memories closing. And I feel the harsh inevitability of life's certain change, death, pain, and grief.

But before I turn and leave, I am given the gift of one last remembrance, one last vision to carry into the present to hold and savor.

It is evening in my memory. I am kneeling in the living room. The lights are low, the night is quiet. Papa, Mama, and I read Scripture together and pray. Then Mama tucks me into the big double bed and piles quilt after quilt on top of my small body. I feel safe, secure, and so beautifully loved.

But before drifting to sleep, I peek above the quilts and peer out the bedroom window. As always, my eyes search the large yard for the cherished sight of it. And, there, glowing in the moonlight it stands. The silver rock. How often I climbed on its smooth top to sit and pray and dream the dreams that young girls dream.

Papa had happened on the rock one day long ago, and he had challenged his strong, robust new sons-in-law to pick it up and put it down—right in the middle of his front yard. There, solidly and firmly planted it had stood, glowing in the moonlight for decade after decade.

"Mommy! Mommy!" I hear the sounds and calls of playing children, and I realize they are no longer sounds from the past but from the present. I close the mental album and I leave the past. But before I do, I turn once more and catch a final glimpse of the little dark-haired girl frolicking in the sunshine.

But, alas, the child is gone forever. She has become a woman with young children of her own, children who will never know the sounds, smells, and joys of Mama and Papa's farm.

As I pull my car out of the driveway, I notice the rock. The silver rock. It's the only thing on the farm that hasn't changed. There it stands, its head held as high as ever, still solidly planted in the front yard. And I am sure, as I drive out of sight of the house and yard and hickory trees, that with each passing night for decades to come, the silver rock will be right there, glowing with each new moonlit night. And I feel a touch of hope.

The Pain of Change

Pain is not a subject I enjoy writing about. Yet if we as Christians are to acknowledge Him in *all* ways (Prov. 3:6), I cannot leave a giant gap in this book and conveniently skip over the subject of acknowledging Him in our pain. If God allows us to become tender to Him in *all* ways, then He also allows us to become tender to Him in our pain.

Pain can be creative and destructive, ennobling and embittering, protecting and destroying, good and evil. In the midst of physical and/or emotional suffering, we usually will cast pain in a negative light. But some of the greatest lessons I've learned in life have been taught to me by Pain the Teacher. Usually, it is only in looking back on the suffering that I realize and better understand the growth that resulted from it. I have a high opinion of pain as an effective teacher of spiritual maturity, wisdom, and appreciation.

"Pain makes man think," wrote John Patrick in *The Teahouse of the August Moon*.

Indeed.

Pain also makes the Christian ask questions, deep probing questions aimed directly to all-loving, all-powerful,
Almighty God. Sometimes pain will make the Christian's
hand ball into a tight, angry fist, a fist that shakes itself
toward heaven.

God did not intend it so. His original plan did not include a world that groans in pain. Yet it is a fallen world,
a tainted creation, a world engulfed by toughness and sin
and touched with pain.

I find it interesting how pain has been perceived
throughout history. In Jesus' time, for instance, people
believed pain was a form of punishment for sin. That be-
lief still exists among many today. In fact, the first definition for pain in *Webster's Ninth New Collegiate Dictio-
nary* is "punishment."

Interesting. Indeed, some of the crazy things we hu-
mans do can cause much pain to ourselves and others. We
may suffer pain as a result of our unwise decisions and
wrongdoings. But Jesus made it quite clear that pain is
not a punishment God heaps upon us because of our sin.
In the Old Testament, Job committed no known wrong
when he suffered so. And when Jesus' followers asked
Him why the blind man Jesus healed was born blind,
Jesus told them, "It was not that this man sinned, or his
parents, but that the works of God might be made mani-
fest in him" (John 9:3).

Pain inflicted by one human being on another is unthinkable to me. It's one thing to endure pain caused by
disease or accident—those crises insurance companies
have named "Acts of God." It's quite another thing to
bear the pain caused by another. Every day we hear the
cries of the children, the unborn, the women, the men,

and the elderly who become victims of someone's cruelty. How anyone can hurt another person lies beyond my understanding.

Yet, even in those unfair and cruel circumstances, God can bring spiritual growth and strength.

I am reminded of the tender story told by Shirley Dobson, wife of Dr. James Dobson. Tears came as I listened to the tape in which she addressed a large group of Sunday School teachers.

Mrs. Dobson told about growing up with an alcoholic father, a father who became violent when he drank and who spent entire weekly paychecks on alcohol. I heard her express the pain of her childhood, how she had yearned for a normal home like her schoolfriends, and how her homelife had produced deep scars in her.

Fortunately, however, like many others in the same circumstance, Mrs. Dobson had a turning point in her life. Through the words of a Sunday School teacher, she gave her life to Christ. Her alcoholic father later left the family, and her mother married a man Shirley admired and loved.

Remarkably, today Mrs. Dobson is able to look back over a traumatic childhood imposed upon her by an alcoholic father and see the spiritual strength it gave her. "My circumstances in my childhood helped me to find and to depend on God," she stated. "It just could be that your past circumstances and your present circumstances may be the very vehicle that God is using in your life to help you to depend on him."[2]

Time and again I hear people tell stories of hard and painful childhoods. But some are not able to erase the pain and begin again. They either don't know or don't trust the strong, solid Rock they can hold onto in times of trouble. They are tossed and mauled by waves too strong, too fierce for their frail bodies to swim against. And they sink.

I've met many others, however, who with God's help have overcome painful childhoods. Like Mrs. Dobson, they have allowed all of life's unfair cruelties to turn them toward God and to make them strong in Him.

As I proceed to step cautiously into this chapter, please know that I don't even pretend to have all the answers about the trauma or the benefit of pain. I can only share with you what I myself am finding, and what others have also found to be true.

Crisis and Change

Crisis and change. They are certain in this life. Someone once said: "The only thing that doesn't change is change." Crisis and change can cause our human minds and hearts much pain. And in our fast-spinning, high-tech, mobile world, unexpected crisis and rapid change can shatter our personal world in a matter of moments. Trying to hold onto our way of life is like trying to contain sand in a child's toy sifter. We simply can't. We cannot contain change. We cannot bottle time and experience and cork the top.

My grandparents' farm is a good example of painful and unexpected crisis and change. One day my grandparents walked through the gardens and pulled tomatoes off the vines. The next, they were gone and their flourishing farm was decaying. Those of us who are left must somehow pick up the splintered pieces and once again cope with life in a fast-moving, ever-changing world.

Pain not only teaches us lessons we could not otherwise learn, but pain forever changes us. For once we have looked at the world through tear-blurred eyes, we will no longer be the same. We will have taken a giant step, either backward or forward, but a life-changing step just the same.

Pain: The Inevitable Fact of Life

What I am going to say next may seem like a contradiction. But here goes.

Some of the most angry, lonely, and incredibly unhappy people I've ever met have been people plagued by a lifetime of sickness, pain, and deep grief.

Some of the most empathetic, loving, sensitive, compassionate, and spiritually mature people I've ever met have been people plagued by a lifetime of sickness, pain, and deep grief.

I believe the difference between the two sets of people comes as a direct result of their response to sickness, pain, and deep grief. I've noticed several different ways Christians respond to pain.

Despair and Anger

Some just despair in it. In pain, they take a giant step backward. Anger, frustration, bitterness, and fear are natural stages of grief. Yet stages are meant to come and to pass. Some, however, step back and stay there. They pitch their tent in this stage and forever live there. When they so need to open wide their hands and grasp God's love and strength, they keep their fists tightly clenched.

A Sad Cross to Bear

Some accept pain as a "cross to bear" and try to shoulder the weight of grief all by themselves. They experience pain, but they don't allow themselves to learn from pain. One painful experience after another brings no particular insight or deeper spiritual probing. They may never seek pain as a tool to spiritual and/or emotional growth. They may take a step backward and then step up again to the same place they were standing.

Becoming Tender to Pain

But some people have found a totally new and different way to respond to pain. They take a giant step forward and they become tender to pain. At times, they too despair under the weight of pain or sadly accept it as a burden they must bear. But these people don't stay there. They take pain one step further. They allow pain, every moment of it, to help them grow to new spiritual heights.

In the midst of pain, these people hold tight to the "Solid Rock" (as the wonderful old hymn pictures God), the One who, in an ever-changing world, never changes. They do not suffer alone. In their pain, they ponder deeply, expect insights, and look to God for answers to their urgent questions. They hold onto their faith in Jesus Christ as they move through the stages of pain and grief, always praying, and always looking to Him to bring the promised good out of any and every bad circumstance (Rom. 8:28).

God, help us to remain vulnerable, open, and receptive when hurt wants to draw us into its thick, impenetrable shell. Oh, how comforting the shell is when pain encourages us to withdraw from life, when we attempt to retreat from further pain. But the shell can only close us off to the voice of God that may be speaking to us through our pain, calling us to ministry, calling us to new growth.

Can Anything Good Come from Pain?

"Suffering can be a strong stimulus of growth and development," writes Eugene Walker. "We . . . learn from suffering."[3]

Old Testament Job lost everything he had: his children, his health, his friends, and his wealth. Yet in his pain and grief, when he had nothing more he could lose outside of his life, Job learned a lesson he would never forget, a lesson about the majesty and grandeur of God.

Some of the most beautifully insightful passages in the Old Testament were written by David the psalmist as he lived engulfed by fear and pain and grief.

On and on we could cite biblical examples of people who became tender to pain and allowed it to change them and to grant them greater spiritual understanding.

Some of the greatest books have been written by those who were deeply moved and changed and given new insight because of pain and loss.

Perhaps you've read C. S. Lewis's *A Grief Observed*. After the death of his wife, Joy, C. S. Lewis recorded his thoughts in a journal. At first, Lewis railed against God. "Is God a 'Cosmic Sadist'?" he wrote in anger. "Time after time, when He seemed most gracious He was really preparing the next torture."[4]

For a long time when he tried to pray, Lewis felt God didn't hear his prayers. "Go to Him when your need is desperate . . . and what you do find? A door slammed in your face, and a sound of bolting and double bolting on the inside."[5]

But he never stopped praying. And, in time, Lewis experienced an unmistakable God-given peace that grew stronger with each passing day. Emerging from his tragedy, he experienced a newfound tenderness toward God and a complete rediscovery of his faith. "Grief is like a long valley," C. S. Lewis could one day write, "a winding valley where any bend may reveal a totally new landscape."[6]

C. S. Lewis did, indeed, discover a new landscape at the end of the bend, a landscape of stronger faith in God as a result of his intense pain.

Doug Manning writes: "Grief is not an enemy—it is a friend. It is the natural process of walking through hurt and growing because of the walk."[7]

Pain: The Giver of Insight

Several years ago I asked twenty-one women to each write about a severe and painful crisis they had experienced and how faith in God had pulled them through the crisis.

The women wrote about many different kinds of experiences: the pain caused by breast cancer, unfaithful and physically abusive husbands, the death of a child, the suicide of a father, and many more. I was touched by their tender and revealing stories.

These women had suffered unbelievable pain. While they offered no pat answers, I was amazed at how these women of different ages and backgrounds had harnessed pain and had allowed it to bring them new and profound insights into God. In each case, the woman not only triumphantly survived the crisis, but emerged from it with a rock-solid and strengthened faith.[8]

Growing Spiritually Through Pain

How we respond to pain will determine how we grow from pain. As already noted, pain can be a teacher of spiritual beauty or a teacher of emotional bitterness. Pain has a way of stopping us in our tracks. And if we will listen, we will hear God speaking to us most keenly and most clearly in the very midst of our pain. "One can never foresee the means that God will use to touch a [person's] heart, the roads along which he will drive him, nor the moment at which he will intervene in his life," writes Paul Tournier. "It may be at the height of happiness, or in the midst of a painful crisis."[9]

Through pain, the human body directs us toward a physical need. Perhaps, also through pain, the spiritual body directs us toward a spiritual need. At any rate, pain is an interruption, an intervening into our lives. Perhaps in these painful experiences dawn our most teachable moments, when we are stopped, when our hearts and minds are open and most willing to accept divine insight. If that is true, by becoming tender to the pain instead of becoming bitter because of it, we can learn from it, grow through it, and one day look back on it not so much as an enemy.

I'll never forget Mother Teresa's words shared with me by a friend who heard her speak. "Don't ever waste one minute of pain," she said. I've pondered those words for months. And, in the light of them, two Scripture verses

I've never really understood become more clear: "Rejoice always, pray constantly, give thanks in all circumstances," Paul wrote, "for this is the will of God in Christ Jesus for you" (1 Thess. 5:16-18); "Count it all joy, my brethren, when you meet various trials, for you know that the testing of your faith produces steadfastness. And, let steadfastness have its full effect, that you may be perfect and complete, lacking in nothing" (Jas. 1:2).

The Door of New Vision

I'm beginning to believe that pain and grief can open doors of new vision to us. It can give us experiences that transform our lives and the lives of others who witness our response to pain.

Perhaps one of the most insightful books I've read is John Claypool's *Tracks of a Fellow Struggler*. In all honesty and vulnerability, he records his deepest feelings of pain, frustration, doubt, and grief when he lost his eight-year-old daughter, Laura Lue, to acute leukemia. "As I watched my little daughter suffer, I could see no reason or purpose in what was happening to her," he writes. "The flow of events did not seem to be going in any meaningful direction, and I had my moments when I understood how a man could raise his fist to heaven and curse God."[10]

When he prayed, he experienced the same deafening silence C. S. Lewis felt. "I had done a lot of talking and praying and pleading, but the response of the heavens had been silence."[11]

But John Claypool also experienced a turning point in his anger and grief. The pain of loss opened the door to

astounding new insight, a whole new way of looking at
life. "Life is a gift," he would later write. "And it is to be
received and participated in and handled with
gratitude.[12]

> "It makes things bearable when I remember that Laura
> Lue was a gift . . . something I neither earned nor deserved
> nor had a right to. And when I remember that the appro-
> priate response to a gift, even when it is taken away, is
> gratitude, then I am better able to try and thank God that
> I was ever given her in the first place.[13]

Perhaps at this very moment you are in the midst of
deep pain. You may be suffering because of a physical
sickness. You may hurt with the death of a loved one.
Your pain may be caused by spouse abandonment or di-
vorce or family rift or financial or work problems. I give
no easy answers about the pain you experience, but if you
will, allow me to leave you with some insight into your
pain.

God will stay close to you in your pain, and He will suffer as deeply as you suffer. Know that He didn't cause the
pain and that He is not punishing you in any way, but
that He will somehow, in His own mysterious way and
time, bring good from it. Wait for that good. Watch for
that good. Stay close to Him, lean on Him, never stop
praying. And though it may not seem so now, He is at
work in your pain, transforming you and transforming
others close to you.

Know that your hours of pain are not wasted. Perhaps
it is through this means that God will show you a glimpse

into the real meaning of life. Listen for His whisper. Wait for His surprises. Don't waste these precious moments, but open up to them. Make yourself vulnerable to God, and He will convert the painful moments into teachable moments. The outcome of your situation may not be what you would want it to be, but trust Him in that too. For you are His. You will be changed because of your pain. You will become a different person. If you will allow it, the suffering you now experience can be the agent that will produce in you a stronger and more solid faith, a faith that will one day in Jesus Christ be perfected.

Hold onto the Rock, the solid and firmly planted Rock that abides beside you, loving you, suffering with you, working through you—throughout all eternity.

Notes

1. Norman Autton, *Pain: An Exploration* (London: Carton, Longman and Todd, 1986), 1.

2. (Story by Shirley Dobson, twelve-cassette program with program booklet.) James C. Dobson, *To Be a Woman* (Waco, TX: Word Educational Products Division, 1982), 68-69.

3. C. Eugene Walker, *Learn to Relax* (Englewood Cliffs, N.J.: Prentice-Hall, Inc., 1975), 41.

4. C. S. Lewis, *A Grief Observed* (London, England: Faber and Faber, 1961), 27.

5. Ibid., 9.

6. Ibid., 47.

7. Doug Manning, *Don't Take My Grief Away from Me* (Hereford, TX: In-Sight Books, Inc., 1979), 67.

8. See Denise George, *When Night Becomes As Day* (Nashville: Broadman Press, 1986).

9. Paul Tournier, *The Strong and the Weak* (Philadelphia: The Westminster Press, 1963), 93.

10. John Claypool, *Tracks of a Fellow Struggler* (Waco: Word Books, Publisher, 1974), 57.

11. Ibid., 77.

12. Ibid., 80.

13. Ibid., 82.

I can do all things in him who strengthens me.

—Philippians 4:13

7
Becoming Tender to Ourselves

I once knew a young Christian woman who was attractive, well educated, and a deep and sensitive thinker. She seemed to have everything going for her. But when I came to know her better, I discovered that the gentle, peaceful exterior harbored inside a tempest not unlike Mount Saint Helens. She had within her an active volcano just waiting to erupt.

I don't know much about Beth's (not her real name) background, but somehow she never had, or she had lost, all confidence in her God-given gifts and abilities. She was afraid to interview for a job. She was afraid in her relationships. She sincerely craved close relationships, yet she kept everyone who would befriend her at arm's length. She yearned for marriage, children, and a home, yet she became suspicious of any man her age who would be friendly toward her.

Her physical appearance also disturbed her. When Beth looked at herself in the mirror, she couldn't see a beautiful face, an attractive figure, and a God-given grace. She could only see imperfections, so slight that no one else even noticed them. But year after year she focused only on the imperfections of her face and figure until she intensely disliked herself.

Beth routinely starved herself of any joy in life. She wouldn't allow herself to feel joy or excitement, to play, or to have fun. I rarely saw her smile. She was extremely lonely. Beth had become her own worst enemy.

I have never met anyone as tough on herself as Beth. The last time I heard from her, she had no job, few friends, and little self-esteem. Beth had a very troubled heart.

Becoming Friends with Ourselves

Beth didn't have to live this way. For some unknown reason, she chose to live this way. I tried many times and in many ways to tell Beth what I had discovered in my own life. I tried to tell Beth what friends had tried to tell me over a lifetime. I didn't listen either.

"Beth!" I wanted to shout. "You are a beautiful, gifted, valuable woman. Just look how God has blessed you. Don't be so hard on yourself! Untrouble your heart. Be tender with yourself, learn to love yourself, become your own best friend! Reach out to others and allow them to reach back to you. Stop pushing people away."

I also wanted to tell her that as a Christian, she had the power of the Holy Spirit in her life; that the Holy Spirit would give her strength, encouragement, and comfort if she would allow Him to; that she shouldn't be afraid to interview for a job, or go out on a date, or use her gifts for God; that she could do *anything* in Christ, who would give her the needed strength, guidance, and wisdom.

But I never got through to Beth.

A Troubled Heart

I once had a troubled heart like Beth's. I too had little
self-esteem or confidence in my abilities. I had a tender,
loving heart that yearned to reach out to others, yet it lay
encased within a hide so thick it couldn't reach out. I
yearned for deep, loving friendships, and when they
came, I pushed them far away from me. Like Beth, I built
a prison wall around myself and simply retreated from
life.

[A genuine withdrawer] will spend much of his time alone
and will avoid any activity that might prove threatening.
He will peek out at the world going by, but will rarely let
his hidden self be observed, either publicly or in private.[1]

I was a genuine withdrawer for sure. I was a loner. I felt
I could do nothing well. I had ambition to do something
worthwhile, but that ambition was unfocused and frus-
trated. I had not yet discovered my God-given gifts. I was
wearing a mask, laughing on the outside but sad and
filled with sorrow on the inside. I peeked out at a passing
world from behind a tough mask. And I had drifted so far
away from God that I felt no longer comfortable praying
to Him or spending time with Him.

I too knew about the volcano within that threatened to
blow its top. It produced a restlessness that kept my spirit
in constant disruption. The stress and pressures of everyday living became like a pressure cooker with no safety
valve to let off excess steam. I came to the point that I no
longer wanted to live. I remember well the late night I
prayed that death might lie down beside me and comfort
me in my sleep.

I wrote about this tremendous stress and its debilitating effect on me in the book *Faith for Everyday Stress*.[2] After the book was released, four or five of my closest friends told me they had no idea of the stress I had endured. I had worn my mask well—a mask that you, too, might be wearing right now. And not even my best friends could see the hurt and suffering and volcanic activity that brewed beneath my "all-is-well" smiling mask.

On the Way Back Home

But, like the prodigal son, I found my way home again. I came home, and the Father ran to greet me and welcome me back. I've decided not to leave home again, for I've found a relationship with my Father I could have never before envisioned. And I have discovered relationships with my husband and children and others that have fulfilled me deeply.

Surprising me most of all, however, I have come to realize *I can also have a genuine relationship with myself.* I never knew this was possible. This is a relationship built on the love and honor and respect of oneself to oneself. We come into this relationship with ourselves once we discover just how much God loves, honors, and respects us.

I truly believe that the troubled heart grown lukewarm and colorless can be rekindled by God's love. God can stir the ashes that no longer glow, and the fire almost extinguished can begin to burn once again with new flame. I know this is true because God set this drifter's heart and soul ablaze with a fire that now burns both day and night for Him. Indeed, one can go home again.

The loving tenderness of relationship, demonstrated to me in a most vivid teachable moment by a tough-skinned rhinoceros, has entered and changed my life. I have learned firsthand that genuine relationship with God, with others, and with myself begins with and is built on tenderness.

Becoming Tender to Ourselves

If God so loves us, ought not we also to love ourselves? I'm not talking about a self-love built on narcissism, selfishness, and self-centeredness. Rather, I'm referring to a wholesome self-love that builds within us respect, confidence, and esteem, and allows us to better give ourselves in love to God and to others.

Just how can we have genuine relationship with ourselves? The following list is not exhaustive, but here are a few ways I have discovered to have relationship with myself.

1. *We can learn to love ourselves and forgive ourselves as God loves us and forgives us.*—Perhaps true self-tenderness begins when you and I discover firsthand that we are loved unconditionally by God.

In other words, His love is forever and His love is forever forgiving. No matter what mistakes we make, if we genuinely seek His forgiveness, He will forgive us.

Now I don't believe we should continually indulge ourselves in wrongdoing, ask forgiveness one day, and then again the next day indulge in the same wrongdoing. For instance, if a married woman is involved in an immoral relationship, in order to seek true forgiveness, she must be willing to end the relationship. To ask God's forgiveness for the wrongdoing and then continue the immoral relationship would abuse God's gift of forgiveness.

After we turn away from the wrongdoing and seek God's forgiveness, we must also forgive ourselves for our mistakes. God forgives and forgets. God wants us to forgive and forget too, never mentally rehashing or lashing ourselves again for past mistakes.

Not only is God's love forgiving; it is forever. It will never end. "For the mountains may depart and the hills be removed, but my steadfast love shall not depart from you," God spoke through His prophet Isaiah (Isa. 54:10).

Let His love fill you. Let His love allow you to love yourself. If you have disliked yourself for so long that you think you cannot learn to love yourself, begin the process by loving deeply the One who lives within you. Saint Augustine once said, "Insomuch as love grows in you so in you beauty grows. For love is the beauty of the soul." Allow God's love to so fill you with growing beauty that you will become like the cup of milk poured by the average child—filled to the brim and overflowing onto everyone and everything around it!

2. *We can know we are beloved individuals to God.*— God knows your name. God knows my name. Calling someone by his or her name shows respect for that person. A name makes a person (who is one out of five billion in the world) an individual.

Would God have given every snowflake its own unique design and not given His greatest creation—His human creation—a unique individual design? We are no faceless stranger in the crowd. We are a beloved individual to God with a given name He calls in love.

I learned the value of having a name when, some ten

years ago, I tried to obtain a passport for my first trip to Europe. When I received my birth certificate through the mail, I was stunned. All the correct information was listed, but I had no name. On the line where my name should have been, it simply read: "Unnamed Female."

I immediately wrote to my mother (and, by the way, I signed the letter "Unnamed Female"!) and asked her why my birth certificate didn't have my name on it. She told me they couldn't decide on a name in time to have it recorded on the certificate. I cannot tell you how empty I felt. For the following few days, I felt like a real nobody.

The next action I had to take proved even more humiliating. Timothy had to go down to the courthouse in Boston, Massachusetts, raise his right hand, and tell everyone in the room that I (who stood very much alive right beside him) had been "born alive."

In God's eyes there are no unnamed females or unnamed males. Is it not remarkable that the God who created the universe and moment by moment keeps its wheels spinning knows each of us by our name? We are individuals to Him whom He personally equips with unique gifts, whom He individually calls into vocation for Him, whom He loves, leads, blesses, listens to, and calls by name. He gives us respect, and He wants us to also respect ourselves.

3. *We can strive to grow in deep loving relationship with Him.*—When my troubled heart returned home to the Father, I had new enthusiasm to learn more about Him. I wanted to spend time with Him in prayer, and I wanted to read His Word. Indeed, when we love someone, we want to spend time with him. We want to learn all we can about him.

I also found a hidden treasure in worshiping with a congregation of believers and in spending time with spiritually mature Christians. My relationship with God began to grow, and I came to love Him more with every thought and prayer.

When we become tender to ourselves, we allow ourselves to open up to the Father, to look to Him, and to acknowledge Him in everything we do. Jesus Himself spent much time developing His relationship with the Father. He spent literally hours and hours in solitude, prayer, and study. So deep was His relationship to the Father that Jesus called Him "Abba," an endearing name similar to a little child's addressing her "Daddy."

As we grow in the relationship, Jesus will fill up our heart, our mind, our moments, our very being. For the very heart of being a Christian is to make Jesus Lord of our life.

4. *We can trust God and depend on Him for all our needs.*—A few years before my grandfather's death, he and I talked at length about prayer. I'll never forget that life-changing conversation.

"I need God's guidance in the small areas of my life, but I feel as if I bother Him with all the little details," I confessed to my grandfather during a discussion on prayer. "I pray about the big things, but do you really think God cares about my everyday problems?"

My wise grandfather didn't say a word, but reached for his Bible. Opening it, he read a verse aloud: "But even the hairs of your head are all numbered" (Matt. 10:30). Then he closed his Bible, and with searching blue eyes he looked at me and asked, " 'Nisey, if God loves you enough to count the hairs on your head, don't you think He cares about *every* detail of your life—big and small?"

I had read that verse a hundred times, but until that moment I had never fully understood it. The number of hairs on my head? What could be less important to me? Yet God cared.

After our conversation, my prayers began to change. It took a long time, but I have remembered that Scripture, and I have begun to trust God and include Him in every aspect of my life, even the smallest details. If God could love me enough to care about the seemingly most insignificant area of my life, the hairs on my head, how much more He cares about the little things that concerned me!

That gave me a sense of how very valuable I was to God. If God could love me and give me that kind of value, then surely I could also love and value myself. And loving someone and giving him value is the beginning of a lifelong relationship with God, others, and with ourselves.

5. *We can change the way we think about ourselves.*—A tough world may be telling you that if you don't meet its materialistic criteria, you aren't worth much, have no place here, will never amount to anything, and so on. But Paul had an answer to this problem. He wrote, "Do not be conformed to this world but be transformed by the renewal of your mind, that you may prove what is the will of God, what is good and acceptable and perfect" (Rom. 12:2).

In other words, don't listen to what a tough world tells you. You don't belong to the world; you belong to the Lord. And if you want a transformed life, you can change your life simply by changing your mind about yourself and your life.

What is your present opinion of yourself and your abilities? Do you look in the mirror every morning and tell yourself you're a real loser? Or that you're ugly? Or that you're a failure? Maybe you've had, or now have, someone who drilled that into your head until you've come to believe it.

Well, stop up your ears and don't listen to it anymore. And don't believe it anymore either. You aren't a loser, or ugly, or a failure. "In heaven's eyes," Sandi Patti sings, "there are no losers." Or as the popular poster pronounces, "God don't make no junk."

I remember the time my grandfather asked me to say his favorite verse in the Bible, John 3:16. Instead of saying "God so loved *the world,*" he told me to put my own name there. I did and it went like this: "For God so loved [Denise] that he gave his only Son, that whoever believes in him should not perish but have eternal life." Then Papa told me that had I been the only person on earth in need of God's love and grace, He would have come, and He would have given His life just for me.

If that powerful statement of love and confidence doesn't change our thinking about ourselves, then nothing will.

Whenever we feel the impulse to verbally wound ourselves, let us look in the mirror and instead verbally affirm ourselves, putting our name in John 3:16. After three or four continuous weeks of self-affirmation, the subconscious, which is controlled by the imagination, will begin to believe what it is told.

"The imagination is the great gift God has given us and it ought to be devoted entirely to Him," writes Oswald Chambers.[3] One of the kindest things we can do for ourselves is to devote our imagination entirely to God and let

His steady affirmation of love and acceptance change our minds about who we are, why we are, and whose we are. Know this: God don't make no junk. He just makes jewels. So consider yourself one of His specially created jewels.

6. *We can change a life-style that's not pleasing to God or to us.*—Not long ago I heard a rather tough interviewer interview a well-known country singer, Ricky Skaggs. The interview went something like this:

"Ricky," she began, sporting a broad grin on her face, "We've heard that your faith is very important to you."

"Yes, it is," acknowledged Ricky.

"Now tell me, Ricky, is it really true that you don't do drugs?"

"That's true."

Disbelief crossed her face. "And, Ricky, is it also true that you don't go out drinking with your friends?"

"That's true."

She looked stunned, then continued. "But, Ricky, don't you ever even have a little 'fling' on your wife?"

"No."

The interviewer sat up, looked Ricky Skaggs square in the eye, and almost blurted out, "Why in the world not?"

Ricky smiled, returned the look, and announced, "Because I just really love Jesus, that's why!"

Ricky's love for Jesus immediately took the poised interviewer off guard. She looked flustered, could think of no response, and quickly called for a commercial.

When you and I come into genuine relationship with God, we are no longer our own. We become a place where the Holy Spirit lives. If we are to listen to and obey His voice, if we are going to love and respect ourselves, then often we must experience a change in our everyday life-style. For those in harmony with God, this change is not so difficult.

Paul told the Christians at Thessalonica, "Test every-thing; hold fast what is good, abstain from every form of evil" (1 Thess. 5:21-22).

Saint Augustine once remarked that if we truly love God we can do anything we want to do. At first his state-ment took me aback and I wanted to say no, no, no, that's not true. But after I thought about his words, I agreed with them. For if we truly love God, we will want to do only those things that would please and honor Him. If we truly "just love Jesus," we will want to live and act and think in Him. In tenderness we commit ourselves to Him in love; and true love, genuine love, brings about different wants. That, in turn, leads to pleasing and honoring God and also ourselves.

Perhaps loving ourselves in Him means saying some loving and firm *no*'s to ourselves. Perhaps loving our-selves means allowing God to shine His flashlight in ev-ery room, every closet, and every corner of our lives.

7. *We can remove our masks and become ourselves again.*—"If I remove the mask I wear, then people will see me as I really am. Is that not too big a risk to take? What if they don't like what they see?"

Before I met a certain rhino, this was the question al-ways on my mind. I have since discovered that relation-ship is indeed worth the risk of removing the mask. Being oneself brings a certain genuineness and beauty. No, not everyone will like the person behind the mask, but that's worth the risk too. We are not called by God to be liked, but to be faithful to Him. Jesus didn't please everyone in

His day, and neither will we please everyone in our day.

At times, for one reason or another, I will allow the mask I think I've discarded to slip into place again. I learned a good lesson not too long ago about allowing that to happen.

I had been asked by a prominent woman to speak to a group of wealthy, sophisticated women in a particular impressive organization. The talk was on the subject of stress; and believe me, I was feeling quite stressed by the time I got up to the microphone.

I had spent hours getting ready that morning. I wanted to impress (my first mistake!). The makeup, the hairstyle, and the business suit had to be perfect. I wanted these women to like me, and for some reason I didn't think they would like me without my artificial mask.

Now, it so happened that one of my dearest friends in all the world had died the night before, and I had struggled all morning to hold back a dam of tears. I managed to keep myself together, smiling and enunciating my words properly until two minutes before I stepped down from the podium.

That's when it happened. That's when the mask I wore slipped off my face, fell to the tile floor, and broke into two thousand pieces. That's when I thought about my dear friend, and, in front of all those sophisticated women, I lost control of my emotions and burst into tears.

Everyone sat there rather stunned in their Liz Claiborne suits and full-length minks and stared at me. I grabbed a tissue, swiped at my tears, and blew my dripping nose. Then I let go and told them about my friend, how much I had loved her and how much I already missed her.

Then something unexpected happened. The women began to pull out tissues and wipe their own moist eyes and blow their own dripping noses. Afterward dozens of women came by, hugged me, and told me their own stories of losing loved ones and the grief they had experienced and were presently experiencing. Later I found out that one woman there had lost her husband just the week before.

On my way out, I stopped in the rest room and glanced in the mirror. My eyes and nose were bright red, rings of mascara made me look like a raccoon, and bits of tissue were stuck all over my cheeks. Indeed, the "perfect" makeup job was gone, but what happened to the mood and spirit in that meeting hall was worth the embarrassment of my tears. For, at the moment my mask fell off, I felt a change come about in the room. I can't explain it, but I remember feeling a great relief.

I haven't since wanted to hide behind the mask. I am becoming more and more comfortable with letting the world see my own face. I am becoming more comfortable with myself.

8. *We can learn to speak kindly to ourselves.*—How often do we speak to ourselves much more harshly than we would ever speak to another person? We criticize ourselves mercilessly for mistakes we made years ago. We even call ourselves unkind names.

When we become gentle to ourselves, we learn the wisdom of Proverbs 15:4, "A gentle tongue is a tree of life, but perverseness in it breaks the spirit."

By speaking to ourselves tenderly, as we would to a child, we build and nurture our spirit and esteem. After all, we are God's children.

9. *We can ask Jesus to move in.*—The church where I am a member, Shades Mountain Baptist Church, has just completed a beautiful new worship center. We've watched the structure go up with great excitement. Not long ago someone turned the lights on inside for the first time, illuminating the large, magnificent rose window.

On that night a mother drove by with her preschooler. Seeing the window, the child shouted with enthusiasm: "Oh look, Mother! The worship center's not even finished yet and Jesus has already moved in!"

When we ask Jesus to move into our own personal worship center—our heart—it is as if a light has been turned on inside us. Those who pass by us can see the Light through our rose windows. They will also see that we've begun to act differently, think different thoughts, and arrange our schedules differently. When Jesus lights up our life, we are no longer the same.

Just imagine how different our lives would be, how wonderfully we would feel about ourselves, if all our words and actions reflected His love for us. If Christ could move in and be the sole motivating factor behind our personalities, problems such as self-dislike, lack of self-esteem, distrust of our abilities, and other dilemmas would find no place to hold onto within us.

10. *We can give ourselves permission to rest, play, and enjoy life fully.*—When we come to love, honor, and respect ourselves, we also will become kinder to ourselves. We will stop pushing our bodies, minds, and spirits beyond their limits. We will begin to walk in rhythm with ourselves, being careful to rest when we are tired and play when we're weary of working. We will give ourselves permission to enjoy life as fully as possible.

When we do this, simple things we're taken for granted since childhood will suddenly jump out at us again, and we will gaze upon them with excited wonderment. God's creation will no longer look the same. We will see it with new eyes. The sunsets, the first spring bloom, the beauty of a child's tender face—we will drink it all in and be more grateful to God for His gifts.

How often Jesus climbed into a little boat and headed for the lake's quiet center to think and pray and enjoy precious moments with God. "Come away by yourselves to a lonely place, and rest a while," He told His exhausted disciples (Mark 6:31).

I once heard my friend and professor, Dr. Wayne E. Oates, lecture on the subject of rest. He told us to follow the example of the human heart. It beats and then it rests, beats and rests, beats and rests. We too should work and rest, work and rest, work and rest. For if the heart should only beat and never rest, it would soon burn out.

When we walk in rhythm with life and nature, we learn to enjoy life more fully. God could have made a drab, colorless world. Instead, He dipped His brush in vivid blues and greens and melons and roses and sunshine yellows and painted the canvas of nature pleasing to the human eye. Then, in His wisdom, He gave us light to enjoy the world's beauty and color, and He gave us dark to rest from the world.

Strive to capture and enjoy the moment of tenderness, rest, and play given to you in the midst of life's toughness. Be kind to yourself, and enjoy the fragrance of the rose God created for you to smell.

11. *We can welcome Christ-centered intimacy from others.*—When we come to truly love ourselves, we will open

ourselves up to the love given us by others. We will begin to know and enjoy Christ-centered intimacy with others. We are created to live in community, not alone. One of the greatest gifts we can give ourselves is to live in intimacy first with the Lord and then with our family and friends.

"Intimacy provides the immune system for the soul," writes Tim Kimmel. "It battles the psychological infections of discouragement, rejection, inadequacy, insignificance, and insecurity."[4]

How can our spirits become discouraged or feel rejected, inadequate, insignificant, or insecure if we are upheld by the intimate love, respect, and intercessory prayers of others? Receiving from others this quality of deep loving expression brings beauty to our souls. Giving this quality of intimacy to others, we discover the gift of genuine love for ourselves.

It is the tenderness in relationship that provides for deep and lasting intimacy in relationship. And since intimate love and tenderness come from God, it is only through Him that we can reach out in genuine love to another. And it is only through Him that we can genuinely love ourselves.

Do you remember the image of the cross I referred to in the first chapter? Jesus is the center of that cross. He is the heart of genuine relationship. All who reach out must pass through the heart of the cross. When God reaches down to us, He reaches down through Jesus Christ. When we reach back up to God, we too reach up through Jesus Christ. It works the same way when we reach out to others and they reach back to us. In all ways, we must first pass through the heart of the cross, Jesus Christ, and He

alone brings about genuine relationship. It is only
through Him that we can find the love needed to genuinely experience a relationship with ourselves.

☆   ☆   ☆   ☆

Beth had a troubled heart. She did not know herself,
she did not like herself, and she had no intimate relationship with herself or with anyone else.

Jesus knew our hearts were troubled, so He came to us
with healing words, words that can mean the difference
between a troubled heart and a relationship built on self-
love, honor, and self-respect. "Let not your hearts be troubled," He told us. "Believe in God, believe also in me"
(John 14:1).

How can we have a genuine relationship with God, ourselves, and others? It begins with a tender heart. Listen to
the wisdom of 1 Peter.

"Finally, all of you, have unity of spirit, sympathy, love
of the brethren, a tender heart and a humble mind. . . .
bless, . . . that you may obtain a blessing" (3:8-9).

Notes

1. James Dobson, *What Wives Wish Their Husbands Knew About
Women* (Wheaton, Ill.: Tyndale House Publishers, Inc., 1975), 32-33.
    2. See Denise George and Steven C. Carreker, *Faith for Everyday
Stress* (Nashville: Broadman Press, 1988).
    3. Oswald Chambers, *My Utmost for His Highest* (New York: Dodd,
Mead & Company, 1935), 42.
    4. Tim Kimmel, *Little House on the Freeway* (Portland, Oreg.: Mult-
nomah Press, 1987), 29.

For whatever is born of God overcomes the world; and this is the victory that overcomes the world, our faith. Who is it that overcomes the world but he who believes that Jesus is the Son of God?

—1 John 5:4-5

8
Confronting the Cripplers

Again and again I hear psychologists report the same list of personal problems common to people today. Although they may list them in different order, the major personal problems most people today face are stress, poor self-esteem, purposelessness, guilt, fear, hopelessness, loneliness, and isolation.

One cannot read the evening newspaper without seeing the effects of these emotional and spiritual "cripplers," for the loneliness and hopelessness is written across the faces of humanity. In some way or another, we are all victims of a tough and confused society.

The world tries to help us decripple the cripplers, but it can only offer humanistic answers. It overlooks the fact we are spiritual beings, created by God with a spiritual base and a spiritual need. We require spiritual remedies.

If we depend on the world for answers, we often spend our lifetimes like caged mice running as fast as we can inside flimsy wire wheels. By the end of our lives, we are out of breath, disillusioned, and wondering why life holds so little meaning. Success measured by the yardstick of society provides little true investment in this life or the life hereafter.

But the Good News Is . . .

Where a tough world leaves off, God steps in. I believe Jesus Christ can release us from those problems that would cripple our spiritual and emotional legs, hinder our spiritual growth, inhibit our reaching out in love to others, and seriously hamper our relationship with God, others, and with ourselves. He can set us free from the burdensome ball and chain we drag alongside us, the bulk that bogs us down and detours us from becoming all that God has planned for us. He can and will give us hope for our lives here and hereafter.

Mosquito or Sledgehammer?

Cripplers affect people differently. For instance, for some, a poor self-esteem might be only an occasional irritation, a pesky mosquito that buzzes around for a while and then goes away. But for others, poor self-esteem can be extreme, and, with the force of a sledgehammer, can crush one's relationships, enthusiasm, ambitions, and dreams.

Cripplers can make us tough instead of tender. They often force us to go through life fighting. Or they make some feel indifferent to life or want to withdraw from life. Often the undiscovered victims hide behind pretty painted masks and become mere pretenders on the stage of life.

Can We Be Set Free?

How can our lives be free forever from those things that would cripple, hinder, and even crush us? How can our spirit be released from the agonizing weight of the tender blockers?

Not long ago in a television interview on what was then my newly released book, *Faith for Everyday Stress,* host Jackie Anderson asked me: "Denise, you aren't a psychologist. What gives you the authority to write a book on stress?"

I responded that, true enough, I wasn't a psychologist; but, perhaps even more important, I was a *victim,* a victim of stress who had found the answer in conquering it.

So I come to you now, not as a psychologist, but as a victim, one who has found, and is still finding, answers to these common cripplers. I have discovered that tenderness removes the barriers, the joy-sapping impediments that, through Christ, I will no longer allow to control my life.

T. S. Eliot once remarked, "To make an end is to make a beginning." I believe that. And in the next few chapters, we will concentrate on how we can confront these common cripplers, bring an end to their nightmarish hold on us, and open our eyes to a bright new beginning.

The world is eaten up by boredom. . . . You can't see it all at once. It is like dust. You go about and never notice, you breathe it in, you eat and drink it. It is sifted so fine, it doesn't even grit on your teeth. But stand still for an instant and there it is, coating your face and hands. To shake off this drizzle of ashes you must be for ever on the go. And so people are always "on the go."

. . . .

The world has long been familiar with boredom . . . such is the condition of man. No doubt the seed was scattered all over life, and here and there found fertile soil to take root.

—George Bernanos
The Diary of a Country Priest

9
The Calling

I once heard Roy Fish tell about meeting a sixty-seven-year-old cab driver in New Zealand. In casual conversation, Dr. Fish asked the man, "If you could sum up your entire life in two words, what would those two words be?"

The man thought a minute. Then, with a look of regret on his tired face, he sighed. "Not worthwhile."

How many other people could look back over their lives with remorse and sum up a lifetime with the two words *not worthwhile*? How very sad.

Reasons vary from person to person, of course, but I wonder if worthwhile vocational ambitions early in life could have been somehow blocked by certain components that detoured dreams and destroyed potential. Key cripplers such as overwhelming distress, poor self-esteem, and a deep sense of purposelessness can block one's ambitions.

While I don't intend to snap my fingers and give quick, easy answers to these complicated problems, I wholeheartedly believe, and I have personally found, that faith in Christ is the essential element in confronting these cripplers. I believe faith in Christ is the beginning, middle, and end to these impediments that block our tenderly knowing God, ourselves, and others in genuine relationship.

Jesus tells us: "Come to me, all who labor and are heavy laden, and I will give you rest. Take my yoke upon you, and learn from me; for I am gentle and lowly in heart, and you will find rest for your souls" (Matt. 11:28-29).

That message is simple enough for a small child to understand and respond to. I also believe that often, if not always, we need a spiritually mature Christian pastor, psychologist, friend, or family member to walk the road of faith with us in overcoming these cripplers.

My pastor, Dr. Charles Carter, once made a statement that has long stayed with me. "You are in the process of becoming forever what you are today—unless you initiate change."

Solutions don't usually happen overnight, but through daily practiced faith, I do believe they will come. And unless we want to forever lug behind us the cripplers we now carry, we must challenge these obstacles and, with God's help, overcome them.

Let us now take a look at some of these common and spiritually debilitating tender blockers.

The Problem of Too Much Stress

We need some stress in our lives just to get us out of the bed in the mornings. But, on the whole, our nation is on the run. Stressed out! We live in the fast lane, driving long and hard until our engines burn out and we are left stranded on the side of the road.

Distress breeds toughness and often makes us want to go through life rushing, pushing, and fighting. An over-stressed life-style allows little time for relationship.

"For most of us," writes Gary Smalley, "our everyday schedules have become so crowded that activity has become a substitute for intimacy."[1]

Constant activity! In this harried, hectic, fast-food society, we eat on the run, work on the run, play on the run, and even run on the run! It's the American way of life.

It's no small wonder that we're depleted physically, mentally, emotionally, and spiritually. Living in constant stress is like trying to pour water from a pitcher without ever refilling the pitcher. It soon becomes depleted, empty.

A few weeks ago I had the "exciting" adventure of helping my seven-year-old put together an insect science project for school. To my relief, he bypassed tarantulas, centipedes, and scorpions and chose to study ants. As we read about the habits of ants, we were fascinated at what wonderfully industrious creatures they are. But we also discovered that if an ant gets sidetracked from his trail, he will inevitably start running around in circles, his industry stopped, his valuable energy expended on a worthless feat.

Living with too much stress is like running around in endless circles. We can so easily become sidetracked from our God-created potential and squander a lifetime expending valuable energy and accomplishing little worthwhile. And all the while we're running, we lose opportunities to love, to know, and to enjoy another in fulfilling, soul-satisfying relationship.

What Can We Do About Too Much Stress?

Distress is an inevitable part of our lives. I'm afraid stress is here to stay. But, by incorporating into our lives quiet times of prayer, Scripture reading, Christian meditation, retreats in solitude, spiritual contemplation, personal and corporate worship, and Christian family and friends, I have found much relief from the aggravations caused by daily stress. I have also discovered that as faith takes a front seat in my life, stress has been forced to take a backseat.

As we begin to center our lives in Jesus Christ daily, coming to Him and asking Him for promised rest, we will begin to respond much differently to stress.

I came to understand this more fully when I researched and wrote *Faith for Everyday Stress* along with Steven C. Carreker. Allow me to share an insight with you from the book.

Having everyday faith is like climbing a staircase. We don't arrive at the top stair overnight. But we take it step by step. With each step we grow in and build up our faith, moving one stair at a time closer to Him, becoming daily more centered in Christ.

In close relationship with God, daily harassments don't fluster us as much. Sometimes we don't allow them to fluster us at all. They come less like floods that threaten to uproot us and more like stubborn cows who step across our train track and detain us temporarily.

God's wonderful surprise to us, in our discovery of an everyday faith, is this: While everyday faith will not remove all the stubborn cows from our tracks, it will change the way we respond to those cows! *Staying close to Jesus*

Christ hourly will drastically transform the way we re-
spond to everyday stress.[2]

Jesus calls us to rest and peace from life's stresses.
Freedom from distress allows us to become more tender
in a tough world, to enjoy meaningful relationships, to
rest and let God alone guide us as we walk with Him into
our future. God can turn stress into energy to be used for
Him.

When we move throughout our day with our eyes planted firmly on Jesus, He will direct us to use our limited
energy wisely, to reach toward the goal He has chosen for
us. We will be given power to accomplish what we could
never accomplish alone.

Peter focused his eyes on Jesus and walked on water! It
is only when we take our eyes off the Lord that we get
sidetracked, begin to run in endless circles, and sink back
into the sea of stress.

The Problem of Poor Self-Esteem

Another tender blocker I have fought most of my life
has been a poor self-image.

In a world so large and crowded, we can easily feel insignificant and inferior. Perhaps within each of us lives a
child who feels afraid and inadequate, a child who builds
protective walls around herself in the midst of a tough
world. Our innermost tender selves can feel like the
small, delicate violet that can be so easily crushed by the
heel of unkind remarks, dubious glares, and biting criti-
cism. Poor self-esteem can make us want to withdraw
from the world into sequestered seclusion or become part
of groups with whom we would never otherwise associate.

Only last week I read this surprising statement: "Studies show that about 90 percent of those involved with Satanism are teenagers. . . . Most teens who become involved have a low self-esteem. . . . The main reason [they] get involved with the occult is that they're searching for some meaning in their lives."[3]
People who harbor a poor self-image are usually unhappy people who look to others in order to form opinions about themselves. They are constantly comparing themselves with others, and they feel they don't measure up. The person who feels painfully worthless only yearns to be loved deeply by someone and to belong to something worthwhile.

What Can We Do About Poor Self-Esteem?

Last week, in a dresser drawer stuffed with old papers, I found a red-rosed birthday card sent to me by my grandparents on my fourteenth birthday. Inside, the tenderness of their words touched me with new strength. "Happy Birthday, Dear. You are precious to us."

As I closed the card and returned it to the drawer, I pondered the beauty of those loving words and how, twenty-four years later, someone who loved me could speak to me with new intensity.

Words are a powerful means of communication. They can control, bless, make, or destroy a life. Careful words from another can build up our esteem. But careless words can knock it down like a runaway bulldozer.

God's words to us are careful words. Again and again throughout the Scriptures, He sends us an uplifting message: "I love you, and I sent my only Son into the world to show you how much I love you. And you can love me back, because I first loved you" (1 John 4:8-10,19, my paraphrase). "In fact, just look around you and you will see that the whole earth is filled with my tender love for you" (Ps. 33:5, my paraphrase). "You, dear child, are precious to me."

Now, I ask you (as I have so often asked myself), how can we have a poor self-image and consider ourselves worthless individuals when the Creator of the universe so deeply loves us? How can we look upon even the smallest wild violet that God meticulously equipped with its own delicate color and scent and not believe that God values us, His most precious creation?

God made us in His own image (Gen. 1:26). And He gave Himself for us so that He could enjoy us and love us and treasure us for an eternity. If we have any doubts about our self-worth, we need only look through the Scriptures to have it immediately affirmed and confirmed. We are a called people—called by God, called to God.

Only after I was finally convinced that I was loved by God and that I had value to God did I begin to grow a healthy self-image within myself.

The Problem of Purposelessness

A sense of purposelessness makes a person indifferent to life. Purposelessness makes one ask: "Where did I come from? Why am I here? Where are I going?"

"There is solid evidence of two powerful undercurrents in our society," states pollster George Gallup, Jr. "1. An intensified search for meaning in life. 2. An intensified search for meaningful relationships, arising out of loneliness."[4]

A person who feels no purpose in life zigzags through life looking for a reason to be here.

What Can We Do About the Problem of Purposelessness?

Late one night I heard my newborn daughter, Alyce, crying in her crib. Half-asleep, I crawled out of bed, stumbled into the nursery, and picked her up. I rocked her, stroked her, and cooed to her, but no matter what I did, I couldn't seem to quiet her. Only half awake, I tried laying her in the crib on her stomach and gently patting her back. But still she cried. At that point I couldn't think of anything else to do. I rubbed my sleepy eyes and looked down squarely into the crib, trying to figure out what was wrong. That's when I saw my weary hand patting the back of Alyce's baby doll. The next morning Timothy and I broke into laughter as I told him how, for fifteen minutes, I had rocked, stroked, and patted a doll instead of Alyce!

Now, we can go through life "patting" the wrong purpose. We can so easily give our attention to that which is worthless and completely ignore that which is of greatest worth. We can mother the doll while the baby goes neglected. We can work a lifetime at a job the world sees as valuable and successful, but one that does nothing to help us grow spiritually or that reaches out to help others grow spiritually.

Most often what the world considers worthwhile and what God considers worthwhile are two different extremes. God puts little value in those things the world puts the most value on, including money, power, prestige, and fame. In fact, I wouldn't be at all surprised if *success*

shouldn't be kicked out of the believer's vocabulary alto-
gether and perhaps replaced with the word *faithfulness*.
For it is in our being faithful to God that we find vocational "success" and purpose.

I find it interesting that the Latin word for career is
vocatio. It means much more than a successful career. It
means a calling into career, a higher calling, even a divine calling into work that will glorify God and serve
others.

When God calls us to *vocatio*, He takes into account our
personalities and gifts. He also gives us the power of the
Holy Spirit to equip and strengthen us in our divinely
chosen vocation. When we heed and follow, we discover
God-given gifts we never knew we had. And when we develop and polish and use our gifts for Him in vocation, we
gain a new sense of purpose for our lives. Our lives become worthwhile as they could never have without Him.
In Him, we can have a vocation that will become a magnificent vocation!

"The greatest use of life is to spend it for something
that will outlast it," wrote William James. What could
outlast our brief lives more than heeding Jesus' words in
Matthew 28:19: "Go therefore and make disciples of all
nations."

I believe that as followers of Christ, we have been en-
trusted with communicating and spreading the gospel.
God calls each of us to this life's vocation and expects us
to use the gifts He has given us to bring the world's others
to Him.

Discovering Your God-Given Gifts

When God called me into vocation for Him and showed me my God-given gifts, I thought I had not heard Him correctly. For one thing, I didn't believe I could do *anything* well. For most of twenty-eight years, my self-esteem had hovered somewhere below sea level. As I stood there with my mouth open, God put a pen in my hand, stirred the fires of opportunity and desire, and sent me a first-class writing teacher!

Then he told me, "Write, Denise, write!"

"But, Lord," I questioned, "who in the world would want to read what I write?"

"Just do it, Denise. I'll be beside you."

So I started to study about writing, to read what others had written, and to write. And bingo! I discovered God had given me the desires, the ideas, and the opportunities to write. Before long I felt like Annie Dillard when she saw, for the first time, the tree with the lights in it.

"I had been my whole life a bell," she exclaimed, "and never knew it until at that moment I was lifted and struck."[5]

I too had been a cold, silent bell, and for the first time I was lifted and struck and I discovered my purpose in life.

And I started to ring! My typewriter hummed ten hours a day and I could see a lifetime of doing nothing but writing, writing, writing.

But just when the typewriter keys began to fit my fingertips, He called again.

"Denise," He said. "I'm going to give you two of the most beautiful, active children I've ever created. You just won't believe how wonderfully active these kids will be!

Mother, Denise, mother."

I had always wanted to be a mother. "I'm thrilled to become a mother, Lord, but You know I've never even changed a diaper. How will I manage such a responsibility?"

"Just do it, Denise. I'll be beside you."

So, with pen still in hand, Bang! Bang! two healthy (and yes! wonderfully active) babies appeared on the scene, and I began mothering. I could see a lifetime of doing nothing but writing and mothering.

But just when I began to get the hang of balancing two babies and a typewriter on my knees, He called again.

"Oh no!" something within me whispered. "What's next?"

"OK, Denise, I've got another job for you. This one will be the hardest job yet. Speak, Denise, speak."

This calling was more than I could handle.

"Me, Lord, a ... a ... a ... speaker? Surely, Lord, you've got to be kidding! Me? Speak in front of live people?"

I couldn't imagine such a thing! "Lord, what about that shy streak down my back that runs from head to heel? And don't you remember how I could never give a book report in school? And how when the teachers called my name in class, I'd suddenly have a shy attack and my vocal cords would freeze?"

"Just do it, Denise. I'll be beside you."

To my great concern, speaking invitations started to come. I would close my eyes, grit my teeth, and say yes before I changed my mind.

And it proved disastrous. The first time I spoke, I tripped over my own two feet on the way to the platform. Then I whispered my entire talk. Even with the microphones turned up full blast, not even those leaning forward on the front row, and straining, could hear a word I said. No one shook my hand. No one said "Come back!" On the way out I promised myself I would never do *that* again!

Only by reason of insanity did I accept another speaking engagement. This time I spoke to a Methodist women's group. They asked me to bring a twenty-minute program. I wrote up my twenty-minute speech and did OK in front of my bedroom mirror. But when real women began filling up the room, I read the thing off like a professional speed reader. I did not once look up from my paper, and the torment (for all of us) lasted only three minutes. Then I folded my speech, stood there red-faced with mouth zipped, and watched the embarrassed hostess try to fill seventeen minutes of silence.

To my surprise (and horror), the speaking invitations kept coming. During those first few years, I must admit to you, I spoke with fear and trembling, and I was never invited back to speak to the same place twice! I am thoroughly convinced the Lord had to be the One churning up those first invitations. Certainly, it was no one who had ever heard me speak before.

Ten years later, writing and mothering and speaking have become so vital to my life, I don't see how I lived without them. They fill me with unbelievable joy, excitement, and expectancy. They have put an end to my shyness, put a smile on my face, and have brought my self-esteem up to a normal level.

Living the Life of Power and Fulfillment

All of this is to say when God calls you into vocation, He will be right beside you strengthening you and helping you to accomplish His goals. "Lo, I am with you always, to the close of the age," He promised in Matthew 28:20.

When we become tender to the Lord in vocation, we discover an awareness of Him. An awareness that we are never alone, but that Someone is always close to us, walking alongside us. He is the Holy Spirit, the Comforter, the Encourager, the Strengthener . . . literally the "One called alongside to help."

Once we tap into His power, we will no longer be the same. For He will stretch us and help us to burst through the tender blockers. Through Him, we will find the needed courage to change the course of our lives and reach toward the personal and vocational potential He has waiting for us.

Honoring God's call gives our lives purpose, and I can think of no better way to invest a lifetime than in something that will last forever.

If only the New Zealand cab driver had known, perhaps at the end of his sixty-seven years he could have summed up his life with two different words: *vocatio magnificus!*

Notes

1. Gary Smalley, "Foreword," *Little House On the Freeway* by Tim Kimmel (Portland, Oreg.: Multnomah Press, 1987).
2. Denise George and Steven Carreker, *Faith for Everyday Stress* (Nashville: Broadman Press, 1988), 84.
3. Lynn Waddell, "Occult Called Sinister Focus of Today's Counter

Culture," *The Birmingham News,* Sunday, 16 Apr. 1989, sec. 1.
4. George Gallup, Jr. (Quoted from the 1989 "Amy Writing Awards" brochure.)
5. Annie Dillard, *Pilgrim at Tinker Creek* (New York: Bantam Books, 1974), 1.

I am the resurrection and the life; he who believes in me, though he die, yet shall he live, and whoever lives and believes in me shall never die.

—Jesus Christ (John 11:25)

10
The Promise

Stress, poor self-esteem, and purposelessness are not the only tender blockers to genuine relationship with God, ourselves, and others. Guilt, fear (especially the fear of death), and hopelessness run a close second in their ability to frustrate us and thwart God's plan for our lives.

The Problem of Guilt

Most often, guilt results from personal disapproval. We feel guilt when we violate God's rules for Christian living. Guilt is like a long, heavy chain we drag behind us throughout life. With every violation, one more steel link attaches itself to the chain. Pulling such a load takes energy; and even though we try to live a Christlike life, the chain slows us down and saps our energy.

Each link in the chain can represent a different aspect of personal disapproval. We can so easily weight ourselves down in immoral relationships, gossip, lying, dishonesty, impure thoughts, self-hatred, envy, laziness, and unleashed anger. As long as we drag the chain behind us, we carry with us these links that will not let us forget them and that constantly replay themselves in our minds and torment us again and again. They keep us burdened down in continual self-disapproval. All too soon, the chain becomes too heavy to pull. With stooped shoulders and aching back, we become its tired victim.

To be sure, the problem of guilt has caused many a believer great distress. Overwhelmed with guilt and trouble, the psalmist David cried out to God for the wings of a dove so he could fly away and be at peace. But, had David been given the wings of a dove, he could have never flown far enough away to be at peace. For trailing in the air behind him would be the oppressive chain.

What Can We Do About the Problem of Guilt?

Perhaps the two most important words to a believer besides "God loves" are "God forgives."

Do you remember the story of the woman caught in adultery (John 8:3-11)? This woman was dragged out, probably only partially dressed, to the temple where Jesus was teaching. Men had already begun picking up sharp heavy rocks to crush her when someone asked Jesus a question about the law of Moses and what they should do about the woman. A trick question.

Then Jesus did something unexpected. He knelt down and started writing in the sand with His finger. They continued to question Jesus. He stood up, looked them in the eye, and said for the first person present who had never done anything wrong to step forward and throw the first rock. Then He knelt down again and continued to write on the ground.

One by one, the rocks dropped to the ground beside the angry hands that held them, for everyone in the crowd had the need to be forgiven.

We have no idea what Jesus wrote. But we do know that when everyone had gone home, the guilty woman stood alone in front of Jesus. He spoke to her tenderly, forgave her her wrongdoing, and told her not to do it again.

I've often thought about what Jesus could have written in the sand. Perhaps when Jesus left and the embarrassed woman stood in the temple all alone, she looked down at the ground and read the words. I like to think they said something like this: "Child, you have been forgiven. Your offense has been forgotten. Now forgive yourself. Don't continue to waste your life like this, for you are valuable to me. I created you in my image, I have blessed you with unique gifts, and I love you. Live a life of respect and live your life for me."

Instant forgiveness. In essence, Jesus had taken the wire cutters of forgiveness and had freed the woman from her heavy chain. And, perhaps, whenever she relived in her mind the horrible scene, she walked back to the words on the ground and again read the forgiving promise of Jesus.

The Gift

Forgiveness is a gift. The criminal crucified on the cross next to Jesus didn't deserve forgiveness, yet Jesus instantly forgave him; and the thief died with the promise in his heart of life forever with Jesus.

Paul told the church members in Rome to get rid of those things that would cause them to fall into guilt, to get rid of the tender blockers in their lives. Set your mind on the Spirit, not the world, for the Spirit brings life and peace, he told them (Rom. 8:1,6).

God wants to forgive us, God wants us to forgive ourselves, and God wants us to forgive others. "Let all bitterness and wrath and anger and clamor and slander be put away from you, with all malice, and be kind to one another, *tender*hearted, *forgiving* one another, as God in Christ forgave you," wrote Paul (Eph. 4:31-32, italics mine).

Time after time Jesus looked into sad, guilty eyes and spoke the tender words, "My child, you are forgiven." He wiped their chalkboards clean and gave them a new beginning. They could once again lift their heads, straighten their backs, and set their eyes on the face of tomorrow.

And His promise of tender forgiveness reaches out to us two thousand years later.

Truly, God is the God of a second chance.

The Problem of Fear

A tough world can be a scary place to live. Healthy fear is a good thing. It can keep us from walking alone through New York's Central Park at midnight, driving our cars at high speeds, or playing with a loaded gun. Healthy fear comes from God-given wisdom and helps us to keep ourselves, our children, our homes, and our communities safe.

But unfounded fear is not a good thing. Unfounded fear is apprehension that has no foundation. It is the little child afraid of the invisible monster under her bed at night. It is the shadow on the wall that follows us from room to room.

But just as the child's monster *seems* real, and just as the shadow *does* follow us from room to room, unfounded fears can seem very real. In fact, they can lock us in self-made prisons and make us afraid to reach out in God-called tasks or relationship. Unfounded fear can cripple us from becoming what God has planned for us to become. It can keep the butterfly in her cocoon because she's afraid to stretch forth her new wings.

Ten years ago, had someone asked me my greatest unfounded fear, without a doubt it would have been speaking in public. As I said before, the thought of my speaking publicly seemed unthinkable. When I first began speaking to groups of people, I was terrified!

After I had botched more speaking invitations than I care to remember, I found a verse of Scripture early one morning that completely changed my mind about speaking publicly. I came across the verse in 2 Timothy. It read: "God did not give us a spirit of timidity but a spirit of power and love and self-control" (1:7).

I cannot tell you the profound effect that verse had on me. Until then, I had thought I was quite alone up there with my visibly trembling hands and knocking knees. But, after reading 2 Timothy, I understood that I was not alone. God was with me. The Helper, Encourager, and Comforter stood up there beside me and filled me with power and love and self-control. After that, I began to stand and speak with much more confidence, for I no longer felt alone or afraid.

I feel a great comfort knowing I am never alone, that the Helper, Encourager, and Comforter is with me, giving me power and love and self-control to face all my unfounded fears.

I believe we can live our lives without unfounded fear. The perfect love of God within us can cast out our fear.

God surrounds us with enough love to conquer our fears of living. His is a love that has no limit. Not even death can separate us from His strengthening love. And He is always with us. "With the Lord on my side I do not fear," wrote the psalmist (Ps. 118:6).

Perhaps you harbor no fear of living. You have come to terms with unfounded fear. But perhaps you possess an even greater crippler: the fear of dying.

The Debilitating Fear of Dying

Unless faced with a life-threatening accident or illness, some people try not to think about their own death. They simply put it out of their mind. That is, until they are under the bedcovers late some dark night and cannot sleep. Then they may join the millions of others throughout the centuries who have pondered the great question, "Where will I go when I die?" They may become so preoccupied with dying that they cannot fully live.

For the believer in Christ, the fear of dying should be an unfounded fear. Why? Because Jesus promised His believers eternal life with Him. "In my Father's house are many rooms; if it were not so, would I have told you that I go to prepare a place for you? And when I go and prepare a place for you, I will come again and will take you to myself, that where I am you may be also" (John 14:2-3). That is the eternal promise from the lips of God Himself.

That verse is so clear, and it gives us needed assurance of where we will spend eternity. Yet, even though we are sure where we are going, the fear of dying itself can still be a great crippler to living. "Just how can I cast the fear of dying out of my life?" I'm glad you asked.

"I'll Be There to Meet You"

I heard a pastor tell an endearing story that has helped me with my own fears of dying.

"I once knew a little girl," he began, "who was afraid to travel by herself to her Aunt Sarah's in a distant city. She had never been there before, and arrangements had been made for her to go.

"Her friends told her not to be afraid, but Jenny was terrified. Then her wise mother spoke. 'Jenny,' she began, 'Aunt Sarah told me to tell you she would be waiting at the train station. When your train stops, she will meet you, take your hand, and lead you to her home. Jenny, you know and love and trust Aunt Sarah. She made you a promise, and she has never lied to you before. So don't be afraid. Just trust Aunt Sarah to be there.'

"And suddenly Jenny was no longer afraid to travel alone."

Jesus has made us a promise. He will be waiting for us when we embark on our long journey, the inevitable journey from life to life. He will be waiting to take our hand and to lead us to our new home. We know Him, we love Him, and we trust Him. We can simply trust Him and not be afraid.

I can also remember, as a young girl, talking with my spiritually perceptive grandfather about my own fear of dying. His words encouraged me so much. He first told me that as a believer and follower of Jesus Christ, I would not die. For sure, I would one day leave life as I knew it now, but I would never cease to live.

He then asked me a pointed question. "Would you be afraid of dying, 'Nisey, if someone you knew and trusted died and then came back and told you not to be afraid of dying?"

"No, Papa," I replied. "I guess I wouldn't be."

"Well," he smiled, "that's just what Jesus did. He died, and then He came back from death because death couldn't hold Him. And He told us not to be afraid because one day we would be with Him throughout eternity."

Many years later, when Papa faced his own death, I thought about that conversation. And I felt assured that when Papa gently went to sleep on his last night, Jesus met him at the station and tenderly took him home.

Life, A Series of Journeys into the Unknown

We cannot relate well to God, others, or to ourselves when we have the constant fear of dying hanging over us like a dark thundercloud threatening a storm.

The believer in Christ and the world see death so differently. The world believes we are currently living when, in fact, we are currently dying. The world's definition of death is the believer's definition of life. Death isn't the enemy but the gatekeeper to a new way of living.

I'd like to close this chapter with a letter my husband, Timothy, wrote to our son, Christian, before Christian was born. After I read this letter, I began to understand better that life is a series of journeys into the unknown. We are always stepping into new territory. Death is simply another such journey.

Timothy's letter is titled "Life After Life."

Dear Little One:
Surrounded in my early childhood with elderly adults, I

first learned about death while still a small boy. Aunt Rene, who was really my great-great aunt, died when I was just three or four. One of my earliest memories is of her wake and funeral. Then there was Aunt Hattie, Uncle Robert, and Dad, all of whom died before I had become a teenager. Sooner or later everyone has to face the reality of death.

So far as we know, of all the species on earth, only human beings can anticipate their own death. Like all living creatures we too must die. But unlike any other living creature, we know this. We think about it, expect it, plan for it. The burden of this foreknowledge can be intolerable. But it need not be so, for death is also a part of life and the gateway to a mystery greater and more wonderful than anything we have known before.

Why do people die? That question is as old as the human race. To answer it completely would be to remove in large measure the mystery of death. There is something tragic about death, despite our modern efforts to smother its ugliness in perfumed funeral parlors filled with freshly cut flowers.

The Bible teaches that death is linked with sin (Rom. 6:23); it is an enemy to be overcome (1 Cor. 15:26), a bondage from which we must be freed. To be sure, death can also be a release, as when someone has suffered for long years with no relief. But there lingers within us all the suspicion, the hope, the whisper of life after death, the "intimation of immortality" as Wordsworth called it.

What is it like to die? Where are those who have died? Christians believe that Jesus' death and resurrection has decisively affected our own destiny. Paul admonishes us not to sorrow as those who have no hope, for to be absent from the body is to be present with the Lord.

"With the Lord": that's the only sure answer we have

when we stand at the graveside of a loved one, when our grief is more than we can bear—they're with the Lord, in his presence, in his care, enfolded in his infinite comfort.

So what is it like to die? Suppose I could somehow get your attention, Little One, make you understand me, as you are now in your mother's womb. Suppose I were to say to you: "Dear Little One, in a few weeks you are going to be born. A life of excitement, joy, and love beyond anything you have known awaits you on this side of birth."

But you respond: "I don't want to be born. I like it in here. I'm warm, I'm comfortable. All of my needs are being met. I've never been born before. I'm afraid to be born."

But then you are born. You discover a wonderful world of color and sound, of music and toys and friends, a mom and dad who love you more than anything else in the world. And you think: "Oh, this is so much better than before." The years go by, you grow up, get married, have children of your own, eventually even grandchildren. Life is good.

Then one day you notice a gray hair in the mirror, your step is a little slower, your memory is not quite as quick as once it was. And you realize, "I'm going to die. I don't want to die. I've never died before. I love this world, my family and friends, my work. Why must I leave them now?"

But then you do die. Suddenly you discover: "Why, this is wonderful. It's just like being born!"

Jesus said: "I am the resurrection and the life; he who believes in me, though he died, yet shall he live, and whoever lives and believes in me shall never die" (John 11:25).

With love,
Dad[1]

And this is His promise to us, His promise of hope. May

we never allow the fear of death to block us from becoming tender to life.

Note

1. Timothy and Denise George, *Dear Unborn Child* (Nashville: Broadman Press, 1983), 85-87.

What I want to say to you is very simple. You all know that a little word from my teacher's hand touched the darkness of my mind, and I awoke to the gladness of life. I was dumb; now I can speak. Teacher credits my hard work, but I know I owe this to the hands and hearts of others. It was through their love that I found my soul and God and happiness.

Don't you see what this means: We live by each other, for each other. Alone we can do so little. Together we can do so much.

Only love can break down the walls that stand between us and our happiness. I lift up my voice in love and joy and the promise of life to come. This is my message of hope and inspiration to all mankind.[1]

—Helen Keller

11
Becoming Tender to Others

[We are] called to bless [others], and to set the angel in us free.
　　—Harriet Beecher Stowe

Not long ago, about fifteen miles from my home, emergency medical technician Rick Harris failed in his efforts to save a newborn's life.

A woman collecting aluminum cans had found the baby stuffed in a brown paper bag. Its umbilical cord still attached, the baby girl was covered with ants and barely breathing. She died soon after, and her tiny body remained unclaimed at the Cooper Green Hospital morgue.

When Rick Harris learned that the newborn would be given a pauper's funeral and buried in the county cemetery, he vowed he would provide her a proper burial. "She came into the world hated," Harris said. "I wanted her to go out loved."

Harris contacted many businesses who donated money, a floral cover, a tiny casket, a burial plot, and a funeral service. The baby received the burial Harris had hoped for.

But the grave site had no marker. And markers were

expensive. But that didn't deter Rick Harris. He set up a fund to raise money for a proper marker. He raised seven hundred dollars, but that wasn't enough to buy the marker he wanted. With the further help of business owners and community friends, he was finally able to purchase the kind of marker he thought the baby deserved.

But the baby had no name to put on the marker. So Harris named her Baby Hope, "in hope that the tragedy would be the last of its kind."

Today, if you visit the Forest Hill Cemetery in Tarrant you will see the graceful marble monument with the praying child angel on top. It is inscribed: "Baby Hope, October 19, 1988, Safe in the Arms of Jesus, Given in Love by E.M.T.'s and Friends."

The monument is a tribute not only to a child who lived a short and tragic life, but to a man and a community in Tarrant, Alabama, who cared enough to reach out in love to a child they never knew.[2]

To Love One Another

"Beloved, let us love one another; for love is of God . . . God is love, and he who abides in love abides in God" (1 John 4:7,16).

God Himself is the giver of love and relationship. His love is like the sunshine, intense and bright. We are nourished and warmed by it. It sustains our very life. And we who live in God are like the glow of the moon. We reflect His great love to others. A loving reflection can uplift the despairing and lonely heart of another.

A few days ago I received an unexpected phone call

from a friend who lives out of state. He called to say hello, to ask how I was doing, and to tell me he prayed for me that morning.

What had started out a hectic, harried day took a different route. My day became transformed by the beauty of his thought, a thought expressed in only a few well-chosen words. I decided to write him a note. I never sent it, but my words were sincere.

Dear Friend:

You stopped the routine of a busy schedule to call me with the uplifting message of treasured friendship. Thank you for calling. Thank you for your prayers.

When you called, you had no idea the problems and pressures that were beginning to mount upon me so early in the morning. A conflict with the children, a load of unorganized work to weed through, a sense of being pulled in all directions.

But it all seems to make better sense now. You showed me what is really meaningful in this life of clutter and conflict. Relationship. Friendship gives the glow to my day. An understanding, uplifting friend gives me the encouragement I need to face a busy schedule. How hopeful to know someone in this impersonal world is thinking about me at this moment and is treasuring my friendship.

Thank you, Friend.

Reaching Out to Others

When we reach out to others in love, we inspire and release the beauty in others. Reaching out and touching another is like the artist who creates something exquisite from nothing. I've often watched my artist mother dip her fine brushes in oil hues and tints and transform a blank canvas into a masterpiece of color and beauty.

When we reach out to others in love, we reach across eternity. We transcend the ordinary and step into the everlasting. We reach out and feed another the food on which eternity is based. Self-giving friendships are not just for the here and now. Friendships stretch into the forever. They will never end. Commitments do not die. And love is a commitment. It is a commitment to care unselfishly for another, to put his happiness and well-being above our own, to edify him, and to lift him up no matter what the cost to us.

"Love is something you do. . . . Love is an activity directed toward another person. Since it is action, it is a decision—a conscious act of the will, an act of faith."[3]

The words *I love you* involve a price. To love someone as commitment, not as mere feeling, involves a letting go of something. A letting go of oneself. There hangs a price tag to that kind of love. It costs us something of ourselves, that tender, vulnerable self. It opens us up to another being and allows another to see us as we are, not what we pretend to be.

The deepest joy and yet the deepest hurt can come from loving and being loved. Opened up, we can experience the greatest joy or the greatest pain from another, depending on his or her capacity to love us.

Joy and hurt mingle, yet for the Christian, the pain of uncommitted love doesn't stop the loving. It doesn't bar the inner walls and close the heart to future loving. It just makes love deeper. It fills the heart with more compassion and sensitivity. It allows ministry to others who have been victims of self-gain love. For the unbroken heart cannot know the pain of uncommitted love. The unbroken heart cannot be used to spread love's healing balm on others.

I don't believe we are born loving others. "Love is the only emotion that isn't natural. The only one that has to be learned and the only one that matters. . . . Most people can love only in shabby, suspicious amounts: when they speak of love they mean getting it, not giving it."[4]

If we live without sacrifice in our love, we live below the level of our humanness, for Christ's love is bound up in sacrifice. Selfishness has no place, no stronghold, no land to pitch its tent. If we want self-fulfillment, we must understand that it comes only from self-giving, a deep sacrificial caring that reaches out to another and unselfishly gives.

If we don't believe there hangs a price tag on self-giving love, let us look at what the words *I love you* cost God. Ultimate self-giving, unselfish, totally committed love whose gentle hands stretch out across eternity and wait for our hands to enfold within His.

The Praying Hands

A moving example of self-giving love is the story of Albrecht Durer, a great German Renaissance artist.

The young Durer was an impoverished painter and engraver in the year 1490. He struggled to keep food on the table and to pay for his art classes. A dear friend of his, Hans, was also a young, struggling artist. The two struggled together until at last Hans came up with a plan. He would go to work so that Durer could study. When Durer became successful, then Hans would return to his studies.

With Hans's gift, Durer studied in Europe with other great artists, produced priceless paintings, engravings, and woodcuts, and then returned to keep his promise to Hans.

Upon his return, as he entered the small dwelling, Durer saw Hans sitting at the kitchen table at prayer. He noticed his hands, calloused and swollen after years of hard manual labor—no longer fit to create delicate artistic design.

So touched by the price his friend had paid so that he could become a successful artist, Durer reproduced his friend's hands, folded in prayer, and gave this image of self-giving, sacrificial love for the world to forever behold.

A Life Transformed

When we reach out and tenderly touch another, we offer a touch of transformation. Often, so gentle is the reach of another that we fail to even notice it. Looking back, I can remember so many ways in which my grandmother reached out in love to me. The child in me was romping, laughing, and playing and often neglected to stop and to thank the one who smiled in the background.

How many times in the snowy winter months did I take off my cold, wet boots at the back door, only to retrieve them several hours later from the furnace top? They were so toasty warm on my toes that I never noticed how they got there. And how many times did Mama stand in the kitchen long hours making vegetable soup when she should have been lying down? I lapped up the soup, my favorite, and bounced on my way to the next adventure. And who so generously hung on the main hall wall my artful attempt at a framed seed and pine cone rooster, even when it brought questioning grimaces from all who entered?

Mama's committed love reached out to me in whispers. Yet, with each whisper, I embarked a bit more into the journey of transformation. In all ways that I can remember, Mama showed me what God is like. For God also reaches out in whispers, so easy to miss, which I bounce by on my way to the next adventure.

I close my eyes and I see Jesus standing on a hillside overlooking Jerusalem. Tears drop down His cheeks and onto His flowing robes as He reaches out His arms in whispered love: "O Jerusalem, Jerusalem, . . . How often would I have gathered your children together as a hen gathers her brood under her wings, and you would not!" (Matt. 23:37).

The hungry child, fresh from sleep, sits at a breakfast table laden with bacon and eggs, toast and biscuits, honey and marmalade, yet refuses to eat.

He came, tenderly touched and healed, fed multitudes, told stories about the Kingdom, offered a higher plane of life with an eternal promise—whispers from God Himself. Yet those whispers were unnoticed or misunderstood. He set the breakfast table, yet the food goes uneaten. His whispers fail to move a handful. He gave Himself in tender, sacrificial, committed love, yet few responded. The world's adventures are too enticing, too captivating, a merry-go-round that drowns out the reality and hunger of life.

What more could God give?

He stands on a hillside and cries: "I offer you a quality of love you have never experienced before . . . a love so good, so tender, its depth will astound and surround you. Yet you settle for such a small corner of love, not even my love, but the world's love, a love that cannot even begin to hold a drop of the great tenderness I feel for you. You accept love that's not really love at all and you reject love that is eternal. Why do you so quickly settle for a piece of coal when I offer you a diamond?"

The Indian Child

Several years ago I had the privilege of worshiping for one week at the Protestant monastery in Taize, France.

Brother Roger, now an elderly, frail man, had founded the monastery decades before. Brother Roger and his fellow monks base their theology and worship on Christ's self-giving love to others. They travel to the poorest spots of the globe and unselfishly reach out to the people of the streets.

During one worship service, I noticed a young Indian girl sitting by Brother Roger's feet. Her eyes stayed glued to him as he read Scripture in many languages and sang chants and knelt in prayer. She basked in his every glance at her. The strong bond of parent-child love was evident between them.

Later, I learned the story of the young Indian girl. Brother Roger had visited an impoverished missionary orphanage in his travels to India. A worker had held up to him the sickly, fragile, dying infant girl with a plea for her adoption. "She will not make it if she stays here in India," she told him. "She doesn't have the necessary immunities to survive India's childhood diseases."

So Brother Roger reached out to her in committed caring, took her as his daughter, gave her a new life in France, and taught her the things of God. Transformation. He devoted himself to her in love, and they became family. So like the gentle reaching of God Himself, who knew that life without Him would end in tragedy. He took us to Himself as His children, gave us new life, and told us about the Kingdom. In Him, we step off the merry-go-round of life, transcend passing pleasures of the next adventure, nourish ourselves from His abundant table, and begin to live life on a higher plane. We meet the Light, and we reflect His light. We become part of His family. And life is never the same.

And the World that Aches with Loneliness . . .

And the world that aches with loneliness aches no more, for in Christ lives no true loneliness. We have His assurance that He will never leave or forsake us. The loneliness we sometimes feel is loneliness based on just that—feelings, not fact. There is a vast difference between feeling and fact. We can't take our feelings in our worst moments as truth. For we know of His presence, which moves and breathes beside us, within us, around us. One in communion within a family cannot truly, factually, be lonely.

But we live in a lonely world, a world isolated from God. A world not as God originally created, but one that, through sin, resulted. The world revolves and aches with deep loneliness. And it need not be so.

The Inner Loneliness

Not long ago I heard the startling statistic that more than 50 percent of Americans admit they are extremely lonely.

A recent survey of three hundred women of all ages revealed that "it's not sex, not money, not good looks that women want most—it's intimacy."[5]

Intimacy, the end of loneliness.

How could this be when in our every waking moment we breathe the air each other breathes, pass each other on busy streets, work together, wait together. Yet we are lonely together. Perhaps we have become a nation of individuals, not a nation of community. Could it be we have learned to keep our arms folded when they were created to reach out?

I once heard the comparison between heaven and hell in simplistic, moving words. Hell, the speaker explained, is a place where everyone sits at a long banquet table spilling over with food. All are hungry. All hold a fork. Yet everyone's arms are ten feet long; and, as hard as they try, they all starve because they cannot feed themselves.

Heaven, on the other hand, is a place where everyone sits at a long banquet table spilling over with food. All are hungry. All hold a fork. Everyone's arms are ten feet long. But everyone is fed because, instead of trying in vain to feed themselves, they reach out and feed another.

I am convinced that if we lived in tender community love, feeding each other, caring for each other, reaching out to each other, we would see an end to the cripplers loneliness and isolation. For it is in the reaching out in tenderness, whether to a deceased unnamed newborn or to a living child, youth, or adult, that we put our love into action.

When we reach out in tenderness to another person, we bless that person and we change that person in some small way. A person is made up of all the people he encounters during the days of his life. Through touching, we become intermingled parts of each other—every person in some way eternally moved by the touch of another. We are each an investment in each other's life, thoughts, and words.

How I remember when friends reached out to Timothy and me during those long years in Massachusetts. The Milleys, the Hughstons, the Allens, and many many more brought us into their family, loved us, enriched us. Deep, mutually loving friendships based on that kind of self-sacrificing, self-giving love never end. They just grow stronger.

Touching the Tough

One Sunday afternoon, after a week-long speaking trip in Fort Worth, Texas, I hailed a cab from the airport to my home.

It was some tough woman who drove that cab. I mean TOUGH. Because she was so stout and strong, I guessed she had been a former heavyweight wrestler! She picked up my two large suitcases, loaded to the brim with books, with her pinky finger. As she zoomed down the highway, her reputation in high gear, the other cabbies all but pulled off the road to let her pass.

As I always do with cab drivers (but this time with some

apprehension), I tried to make conversation.

"Beautiful Sunday afternoon," I called to her from the backseat.

"Ump," she replied. "What's so beautiful about it?"

Not easily deterred, I continued: "Have you had a good day today?"

"I never have good days."

I decided to give up. Tough is lonely. Tough makes fighters. Obviously, she didn't want to talk. But then something made me want to try one more time. Although she wasn't wearing a wedding ring, I noticed a photo of a teenager on the front seat next to her.

Guessing the teenager to be her daughter, I made one last attempt. "Have you and your family lived in Birmingham long?" I groped.

What happened next was unbelievable. She turned around, one eye on the road and the other eye on me, and she poured out a story that touched me to the bone. With huge tears in her eyes, she told me about her life.

She had just moved to Birmingham from New Jersey two weeks before. Her husband had abandoned her and her three preschoolers. Drained of money and with no family support, she had found a job as a cabbie.

She cried when she told me about her lovely teenage daughter, Jenny, whose picture she always kept close to her. At age sixteen and unmarried, she had given birth to Jenny but couldn't support her. With the court's permission, her mother in South Carolina had adopted the baby. While the grandmother would send photos of Jenny, she wouldn't let Jenny and her mother visit. This heartbroken woman hadn't seen her lovely daughter in a decade.

During the remaining twenty minutes of the ride

home, this "tough" woman poured out her story to me, her hurts, her crushed dreams, her emptiness, her loneliness. I could only listen and offer her words of assurance and encouragement. But late that Sunday afternoon, I saw a picture of a tender heart beneath years and years of acquired toughness. And I have many times since thought about her, prayed for her, and hoped for the opportunity to meet her again.

Sometimes when it seems the toughest to reach out, that is the very time we need most to reach out to another. And even though the touch might be brief, often it is lasting. Like the summer butterfly that graces the air for a fleeting moment but leaves a smile on the face of the beholder. A whispered touch that transforms like boots on the furnace top or a morning phone call from a friend. Loneliness cannot live in that atmosphere. Loneliness can only survive on folded arms, hushed lips, and empty hearts.

Perhaps that is the very place Christ waits for us, in those who are lonely, in those who hurt.

To Feed One Another

As I was sweeping the kitchen one spring morning, I noticed two birds hopping around on the patio. The male would pick up a seed from the ground and put it into the mouth of the female. Again and again he repeated this motion, intent on feeding her to the exclusion of his own breakfast.

I believe this is what Jesus meant when He said "Love your neighbor" in Mark 12:31. Feed one another; nourish one another; care for one another.

"Real love . . . is an expression of the deepest appreciation for another human being; it is an intense awareness of his or her needs and longings for the past, present, and future. It is unselfish and giving and caring."[6]

"Walk in love," wrote Paul to the Ephesians, "as Christ loved us" (Eph. 5:2).

And to the Colossians he penned these words: "Put on then, as God's chosen ones, holy and beloved, compassion, kindness, lowliness, meekness, and patience, forbearing one another, and, if one has a complaint against another, forgiving each other; as the Lord has forgiven you, so you also must forgive" (Col. 3:12-13).

What a lesson I need to learn! I can only find that depth of unselfish caring and giving in my Lord Jesus Christ. Only in Him can I take my eyes off myself and look straight into the eyes of needful others. It is a tenderness I can find nowhere else. How I need to take to heart the true meaning of love, as found in 1 Corinthians 13:

> Love is patient and kind; love is not jealous or boastful; it is not arrogant or rude. Love does not insist on its own way; it is not irritable or resentful; it does not rejoice at wrong, but rejoices in the right. Love bears all things, believes all things, hopes all things, endures all things. Love never ends (vv. 4-8).

Only in Christ can we discover and experience this kind of love. For it is beyond us alone. Only God can plant it within us and cause it to grow and flower. Only God can direct us as to when and how to reach out to another. And only God can plant within the heart of another the opportunity for a teachable moment.

Oh, but had one lonely rhinoceros not reached out to me.

The Mark of Love

Real love reaches out to another no matter what the cost to itself. It gives and gives and expects nothing in return. Love can be hanged on a cross and it responds with, "Father, forgive."

Perhaps few true love stories have touched me as deeply as the story of Father Damien.

Father Damien was a Belgium-born Roman Catholic priest who volunteered to minister to an isolated colony of lepers at Molokai, Hawaii.

He arrived on May 10, 1873 and found that the colony had no nurse, no doctor, and no priest. No one wanted to minister to the lepers. So he became their nurse, doctor, and priest. He loved them and touched them when no one else would. He nursed their open wounds, constructed their huts, and built their coffins when they died.

After fifteen years of service, one Sunday morning Father Damien discovered that he had given himself in such committed, unselfish love that he had become one of them. The first sores that appeared on his body proved that he too had contracted the loathsome disease. He too had become a leper. He stepped into the pulpit that morning with the message: "We, the lepers . . ." Not long after, he died there surrounded by those he loved most.

Seeing Others with New Eyes

Something amazing happens to us when God directs our reaching out to others. He opens our eyes and hearts, and we no longer see the leper's sores. We begin to see others with new eyes. We begin to see the heart that beats and bleeds and longs for love. We begin to see with God's eyes. Eyes of tenderness.

We begin to see people the way my late friend, Helen Parker, saw them. Blind from birth, Helen saw people from the inside out, while I, sighted from birth, saw people from the outside in. In our short decade of friendship, Helen taught me more about "seeing" than I learned from a lifetime of sight.

When we see others as God sees them, prejudice melts away. We see with eyes of newfound love. And people don't look the same to us anymore.

Not long ago I wrote a story about the time I learned to see another with new eyes. The story involves an old "town drunk" and myself, a young self-righteous minister's wife. I titled it "The Least of These."

The Least of These

I didn't want to be here. I felt afraid, uncomfortable, and extremely homesick. Sitting stiffly in a metal folding chair in the basement of the First Baptist Church of Chelsea, Massachusetts, I could only half-listen as Larry, a shaggy-headed teenager, read from Matthew 25.

Around me sat nine other tough-looking, blue-jeaned youth. Former drug users, alcoholics, and gang members, each one had recently accepted Christ and had joined our Friday night Bible study.

Chelsea, a poor, crowded, inner city located on the outskirts of Boston, was known for its delinquent youth, drug-selling, and street violence. A shiver passed through me as I contemplated three more years here. After only a few months, I already intensely disliked this place.

As Larry read, my thoughts drifted to the lovely Georgia pastorate we left to come here. After two years there, Timothy had been accepted to study at Harvard Divinity School in Cambridge. He had also been appointed pastor of Chelsea's small mission church.

Larry continued reading. "Feed the hungry, welcome the stranger, clothe the naked, visit the sick . . . Truly, I say to you, as you did it to one of the least of these, you did it to me."

I loved those verses. Years before, my grandfather had put music to the words to help me learn them.

As I played the melody memories in my mind, suddenly the basement door burst open. A cold October wind blasted the room, wildly flipping Bible pages.

An old man staggered inside. He wore a navy blue suit, twenty years out of style. He was covered with city dirt. Wisps of white hair danced around his face, a face carved by years of hard drinking and hostile New England winters.

I recognized him. The town drunk. No one knew his real name, but the street kids had dubbed him "Johnny Cornflakes" because he routinely searched trash cans looking for the last few flakes in discarded cereal boxes. Johnny lived on the streets, slept under apartment porches, and ate scraps of food tossed to him by local restaurant owners.

With stooped shoulders and an age-etched frown, he resembled a Ringling Brothers clown as he limped into the room. He proceeded to step on twelve pairs of feet only to land, amazingly, upright in the chair next to mine. Once seated, he turned his entire body toward me, and, with large bloodshot eyes, he gazed into my face.

Even though he seemed a comical figure, a second of panic passed through me. As a young girl, I had once been frightened by an intoxicated man. Still staring at me, Johnny opened his food-encrusted, toothless mouth and smiled.

The stench of body odor and alcohol hit me full force. I jerked my head away and wrapped my hand tightly over my face. I thought I would be sick.

How I longed at that moment to be back home with the people I knew and loved.

As I struggled hard to keep back the nausea, I remembered the first time I met Johnny. It had not been pleasant.

Two weeks before, on a Sunday afternoon, Timothy and I had given our first dinner party in Chelsea for six out-of-state guests. We could only afford onion soup, baked beans, and my "sweet potato surprise," but we made the table elegant with our silver, china, and lace wedding gifts.

"Just relax, Denise," Timothy told me for the sixteenth time. "I just want our guests to remember this dinner for a long time," I whispered.

Thanks to Johnny Cornflakes, our guests would, indeed, remember this dinner party for a long time. For, just as I served the soup, the front door flew open. And there, in all of his inebriated glory, stood Johnny Cornflakes.

With a grin and a bow, he tottered to the table. Unashamedly, he picked up the silver serving spoon and began shoveling my sweet potato surprise in his mouth. Not knowing what to do, and seeing the horror written on my face, Timothy filled a plate with food and gently led Johnny to the kitchen to eat.

Vividly remembering the dinner party Johnny had ruined, I turned to give Johnny an angry glare. That's when I noticed all eyes on Johnny's shoe. I saw it too. His twisted mass of unsocked foot, crippled by a childhood disease, was stuffed into a shoe with a large gaping hole. Johnny had pushed cardboard into the hole, trying to shut out the blustery New England northeasters.

Larry broke the uncomfortable silence. "You know, it won't be long till winter snow comes. I think Jesus would want us to buy Johnny another shoe."

The others agreed, and immediately emptied their pockets. Larry counted out $15.00.

"This should be enough for a shoe," he guessed. "Let's get Johnny to the foot doctor tomorrow."

I couldn't believe my ears. They were actually going to spend their $15.00 on a shoe for Johnny!

"Well, I believe in helping the poor, but aren't there agencies that could give Johnny a shoe?" I asked.

"With all the papers and red tape," a teenager piped in, "it would be summer before Johnny got a shoe."

At that point, I decided to keep quiet.

The next day Timothy and another church worker took Johnny to the doctor. "Johnny's foot is so badly deformed," he explained, "a new shoe designed to fit him will cost $113.92."

"One hundred thirteen dollars and ninety-two cents? There's no way we can buy that shoe!" I told Timothy later that evening. "Johnny'll just have to live with cardboard in his shoe."

The next Friday night, we told the Bible study group
the bad news.

"Since we can't buy the shoe, let's use the money for
something else," I suggested.

But Larry wouldn't hear of it. "Johnny needs that shoe.
Anyway," he asked, "Isn't Johnny one of the 'least of
these' that Jesus talks about?"

"But . . ."

Larry interrupted me. "We'll just have to earn the
money!"

The next morning, ten teenagers hit the streets of
Chelsea in search of odd jobs. They picked up trash,
moved furniture, and washed windows. It took them six
weeks, but before the November snows came, they had
earned $113.92. And they had bought Johnny's shoe.

It was raining the next Friday night as we admired the
new shoe and waited for Johnny. One hour, two hours,
three hours crept by. But Johnny didn't come.

"Do you think he's left town?" someone asked. "Maybe
he's sick somewhere, or even . . . dead," another offered.

I could stand it no longer. "The old drunk!" I heard myself blurt out. "He could at least come get his shoe!"

Then Larry spoke. "Well, we'll just have to go out and
find Johnny and take the shoe to him."

"But it's not safe to be on the streets this time of night,"
I warned.

But they were determined. So I decided to tag along.

For the next few hours, we crawled under apartment
porches, searched the city's trash bins, and walked the
dirty, wet streets calling his name. But no Johnny. We
finally gave up and headed back to the church.

On the way back, we passed Johnny's favorite

restaurant.

"Let's take one more look," someone said. We walked around to the back and looked. And there, sprawled out in the alley, soaking wet and covered with mud, lay Johnny Cornflakes.

We knelt beside Johnny, and Larry tenderly pulled the new shoe onto Johnny's twisted foot. Then someone offered up a simple prayer for the old man who had spent a lifetime sprawled out in an alley.

Just then the restaurant owner came out carrying a small plastic bag of food scraps. As he tossed them over to Johnny, he hesitated, and then he looked me square in the face. "Here, Lady," he said. "There's probably enough for you too."

As he shut the door, I caught my reflection in the glass. I was shocked by what he had said and by what I now saw. There I was, kneeling in an alley beside the town drunk, my hair wet and disheveled, my clothes covered with mud. The restaurant owner had misjudged me. He couldn't see beneath the layers of city dirt to know who I really was. No one had ever spoken to me like that. An appalling thought came: *He thinks I'm a "bag lady!"*

I looked again at Johnny, who sat and stared at his new shoe. Tears slid down his cheeks and dropped off his stubbly chin. Overwhelmed with gratitude, he couldn't speak. Instead, he turned his body toward me and gazed at my face with those same bloodshot eyes. He then opened his food-encrusted, toothless mouth, and smiled. The smell of body odor and alcohol met my nose, but for some reason I wasn't repelled by it. My hand no longer reached out to cover my face. Instead, it reached out and touched Johnny's face. And, feeling an unexpected tenderness for him,

I smiled back.

"Johnny," I said, feeling the warmth and softness of his skin, "perhaps I have misjudged you too."

Late that night, in a dark alley in Chelsea, Massachusetts, Johnny Cornflakes helped me learn a profound truth. In God's eyes we are all precious and valuable, every person, every "least of these"—whether we be a shaggy-haired teenager, an unempathetic pastor's wife—or an old town drunk with a brand-new $113.92 shoe.[7]

Notes

1. Helen Keller, from the TV movie *Helen and Teacher*, written by Joseph Lash.
2. Carla Caldwell, "Baby Hope," *The Birmingham News*, 2 Mar. 1989.
3. J. Allan Petersen, *The Myth of Greener Grass* (Wheaton, Ill.: Tyndale House Publishers, Inc., 1983), 75.
4. Ibid., 197.
5. Sandra Simpson LeSourd, *The Compulsive Woman* (Old Tappan, N.J.: Fleming H. Revell Co., 1987), 239-240.
6. James Dobson, *Emotions, Can You Trust Them?* (Ventura, Calif.: Regal Books, 1980), 57.
7. Reprinted from an article in *Home Life*, Mar. 1990.

Rejoice in the Lord always; again I will say, Rejoice. Let all men know your forbearance. The Lord is at hand. Have no anxiety about anything, but in everything by prayer and supplication with thanksgiving let your requests be made known to God. And the peace of God, which passes all understanding, will keep your hearts and your minds in Christ Jesus.

—Philippians 4:4-7

12
Wise as Serpents, Gentle as Doves

(Epilogue)

One morning while on my daily walk, I came across a little dog, a golden-coated cocker spaniel. It was quickly evident that the dog was confused.

When he saw me he barked a few times, stepped back, eyed me, and then growled. Then, to my surprise, he stepped forward, wagged his tail, and dog-smiled at me.

I stood there for the longest time trying to figure out this circumspect creature who one minute growled and determined to bite my foot, and the next minute wagged his whole body and reached to lick my shoe.

The small beast stood there pondering the perplexing problem of relational risk. He yearned to step out and find a new friend; yet, at the same time, he wanted quite desperately to protect himself.

I know just how he feels. How many times have I too been confused about risk? Should I stand back, eye, and growl? Or should I step forward, give my hand, and trust? How many times have I longed for intimate relationship, yet, at the same time, felt an overwhelming need to forfeit the friendship in favor of self-preservation?

Oh yes! I've failed to step out and have experienced the unfulfilled potential of friendship. And, oh yes! I've stepped out and have experienced profound hurt by those whose intentions were selfish.

The Baffling Position

It's no wonder we're baffled about risk. It's a tough world out there, and we've got to be on our toes. "Behold," Jesus said. "I send you out as sheep in the midst of wolves . . . Beware of men" (Matt. 10:16-17).

If we choose tenderness as a way of life, then we must step out into a tough world "innocent as doves."

For gentleness is a virtue. It brings kindness, consideration, and sensitivity. Noah chose a gentle dove to send through the window of the ark to bring back news of reconciliation and tranquillity. The dove has long been the symbol for peace.

"Let all men know your forbearance," Paul told the Philippians (4:5). "Aim at righteousness, godliness, faith, love, steadfastness, gentleness," he told young Timothy (1 Tim. 6:11). Give soft answers, advises Proverbs 15:1 (paraphrased). "If possible, so far as it depends upon you, live *peaceably* with all," instructed Paul (Rom. 12:18, italics mine).

But if we choose tenderness as a way of life, then we must also step out into a tough world "wise as serpents."

For wisdom brings understanding, discernment, and good sound judgment. Be wise, Jesus warned, like the snake whose eyes are always open and who is always alert to those around him.

The golden-haired cocker spaniel couldn't make up his mind. No doubt, he spent a lifetime leashed to the rope of indecision. "Should I take the risk? Should I avoid the risk? Should I take the risk? Should I avoid the risk?"

Surely . . .

Surely, genuine relationship is worth the risk. We will not go through life unbitten. But if we don't take the necessary risks, we *can* go through life untouched by human tenderness.

The Christian's aim in life is to touch and be touched. The decision to become tender, while salted with wisdom, is the decision to take a risk on relationship. By offering ourselves up in tenderness to God, to others, and, yes, to ourselves, we embark upon a lifetime journey toward spiritual maturity. We learn of Christ, and we enjoy the fruits of that dependence. The Spirit plants within us seeds of love, joy, peace, patience, kindness, goodness, faithfulness, gentleness, and self-control (Gal. 5).

Through our tenderness, we are given the test of character and maturity, for "one of the most important tests of character and maturity is the capacity of a person to form and maintain *lasting* relationships."[1]

And if we are bitten in the process of tenderly loving another, then we are given the capacity to forgive and to go on loving. For the seeds that are planted within us bloom in tenderness, and the beauty and fragrance of their fruit reach out and reflect the glory of the One who planted them.

For the image of the cross surrounds us, compels us. We push away the "wisdom" of the world and seek instead the wisdom from above . . . the wisdom that is gentle (Jas. 3:17).

It is in Christ's tenderness that we find our strength. It

is in Christ's strength that we find our tenderness. And our previous requests for power become pleas for vulnerability. When our prayers are answered, ordinary life becomes extraordinary. Tenderness transforms our humanness and we experience life on a higher plane, a touch of the divine dwelling within the mundane. A common moth unfolding shimmering wings to catch the light of the sun.

We stretch our wings and we learn of God's ultimate tenderness, the gift of eternity laden with the brilliance of the Son.

How do we become tender in a tough world?

We simply open our hands to God, bypassing the piece of coal and reaching for the offered diamond. In doing so, we transcend toughness. And in the process, we catch an evanescent glimpse of the eternal.

Note

1. Wayne E. Oates, *Behind the Masks* (Philadelphia: The Westminster Press, 1987), 42.